CLONING

CLONING

BY
DAVID SHEAR

 WALKER AND COMPANY ▪ New York

For Joanna and Jason, and for Pat

CLONE (klōn), *n. Biol.* The aggregate of individual organisms descended by asexual reproduction from a single original organism.

·1·

REPLICAS

THE SUN WAS so bright it hurt his eyes, but Paul felt cool. He stood on the sidewalk in front of the department store display window and watched the workmen remove the mannequins. The last one, a little girl, seemed to look right at him as she was lifted and carried off.

Paul entered the store, which was filled with customers crowded around the sales counters. None of them noticed the mannequins being carried by the workmen. He followed them through the store and out the metal fire door into a brick-walled back alley. There was a large trash fire smoldering, and some of the men threw on empty cardboard boxes. Paul remembered that he hadn't seen a trash fire since he was a child, that burning trash was illegal. The men stripped the mannequins, tossing their clothes on the fire. There were no seams visible in their lifelike bodies. They had fingernails and hair and genitalia. Paul looked at their faces, each frozen in a blandly

1

content expression, the glass eyes looking quite real. The men threw the mannequins on the fire, which immediately blazed up. For a moment they were obscured from view, but the fire died down and he saw them melting. Their hair was in flames and there was a sulfurous stench. He turned his back on the fire. The sky had become dark and overcast, and the flames threw a dancing light on the brick wall. Then Paul smelled the odor of burning meat. He turned back and saw the mannequins being consumed by the fire. Their facial features ran and their mouths slowly opened. They began to scream, first one, then another. The little girl was calling for her mommy. He ran to the fire and lifted her out. The flames felt cool on his skin, and he was not burned at all. He looked at her and saw that she was just a plastic shell, now partly charred. She put her arms around his neck and drew her burned face near his. Paul's heart began to race, and he felt like vomiting. He pulled her arms free and threw her back on the cold flames, which started again to consume her body.

Rain began to fall from the dark sky, first a few drops, then a torrent. The fire sizzled and went out, a mixture of smoke and steam still rising from it. The partially consumed mannequins began to crawl from the fire. Paul saw the workmen sitting by the brick wall on wooden crates, eating their lunches. Slowly the mannequins crawled over to the workmen. As they touched them, the workmen froze in place, one with a sandwich a few centimeters from his mouth. The mannequins stripped the workmen and put on their clothes. Then they lifted them up and carried their stiff forms back into the department store.

Paul felt a touch on his hand. The little girl mannequin had taken hold of him. Her face and body were healed, and her touch was warm from the heat of the fire. Paul started to cry. He lifted her and hugged her, and covered her naked form with his jacket. The rain stopped.

Paul opened his eyes. The room was dark. He rolled over and read the luminous dial on his clock. Four A.M. He rolled over again and went back to sleep.

He stood in front of a mirror. Funny, he thought, that a full-length mirror does not have to be as tall as a person. He looked at his reflection and ran his fingers over his beard. A nude young woman with dark eyes and long, black hair stepped from behind him so that he could see her reflection as well. He turned and embraced her passionately. She unbuttoned his shirt and stepped back. He slipped off his sandals and took off his clothes. He could smell her musky perfume. He lifted her chin and kissed her. Their tongues touched gently, and he felt her teeth and the roof of her mouth. They were both breathing fast. She kissed his shoulder and his neck. He placed his hands on her lower back and pulled her close. They lay down on the bed and embraced again. He moved his chest so that it caressed her small breasts. He kissed her thighs and her belly. She dug her fingernails into his shoulders and pulled him up so that he was lying on her. He entered her, a little at a time, and they both drew their breath at each advance. They moved together minute after minute. He raised himself on his hands and looked down at her. Her eyes were closed, her delicate face made more beautiful by the pleasure of copulation. She opened her eyes and looked up at him. She lifted her knees and spread them wide apart. He was in so deep that he could feel her cervix each time he thrust. The intensity of the pleasure drove all thought of equations from his mind. When it came, the climax went on in endless spasms, until they both lay sweating and drowsy in each other's arms.

Paul dreamed that he awoke and the woman was gone. He got up and looked in the mirror. The beard puzzled him since he didn't wear one, and neither did most other men. He reached out his right hand. The mirror felt like a pool of water. His fingers went in, melting into the fingers of his image, followed by his hand and his wrist. He tried to hold back but there was something pulling on him. Slowly his arm and shoulder disappeared into the soft, silvery mire. His head began to slide into the flat plane of the mirror and his vision blurred. There was only blackness. He tried to open his eyes.

Finally he succeeded and was once more awake in his dimly lit bedroom in the real world. The clock said 8:10. The ghosts of his dreams were everywhere about, so he went and drew open the curtains. The bright sunlight and the blue sky over the water of Lake Erie threw him immediately back into the stream of everyday life, and he went in to take his morning shower.

"Suppose you woke up in a room to face an exact replica of yourself, and you each had a knife. A guard came in and told you that only one of you could leave the room alive. What would you do?" Paul took a sip of his Scotch and waited for Michael Jordan to answer.

"Well, am I the real me, or is it the other one?"

"You can't tell. After talking it over, it turns out that you both share all the same memories up to that moment."

"But we couldn't be *absolutely* identical."

"Of course it's impossible in practice, but *assume* that you are."

Jordan screwed up his face. "I couldn't kill anyone, much less my own self."

"Aha! But *is* it your own self? That's what I'm getting at. Remember, you're seeing through only one pair of eyes. Besides, to make the game realistic, say the guard tells you that if you don't agree to play, you will both be destroyed, so you have nothing to lose."

"But I'm against killing on principle."

"Would you have two dead instead of just one?"

Jordan finished his beer and stared at Paul. They were both getting drunk and it was two o'clock in the morning. "If you put it that way, if I were *really* in such a situation, I guess I would choose to fight."

"But you might both kill each other."

"So we could flip a coin, and the loser allows the other to kill him."

"Well. Rationality triumphs. Now what I want to know is, does it *matter* who wins?"

"What do you mean?"

"If you're both identical, the future state of the world

can't depend on which Michael Jordan lives and which dies. Suppose you're the loser. Would you care? Would you be frightened?"

"No. I guess it wouldn't matter."

"Suppose you lose the toss. You see this man, who happens to look just like you, and he's coming toward you with a knife in his hand. Would it really matter whether he was a total stranger or an exact replica? Why would your feelings be any different if it were a stranger?"

"Goddamn it, Paul, you *said* we were identical. Hey, get me another beer, will you?"

Paul walked across his living room to the refrigerator behind the bar and got a beer. He also refilled his Scotch. Through the picture window he could see a few lights on the shore of the lake. He opened the beer for Jordan. "Aren't *any* two humans enough alike so that it wouldn't matter? How much alike do the two people have to be?"

"I guess you're right."

"So you would never fight."

"No."

"Suppose the other man was a murderer."

"If I killed him, I'd be a murderer."

"Suppose he was dying of an incurable disease, and you had the rest of your career ahead of you."

Jordan didn't answer.

"Well?"

"You want me to say I'd fight a dying man."

"I don't *want* you to say anything. I want to know what you think."

"Maybe I would fight him."

"Suppose you had the chance to flip a coin with your own son for survival?"

"I don't have a son."

"I said, suppose."

"I'd let *him* live."

"Suppose he was a mongoloid idiot?"

Jordan stood up. "Oh shit, Paul. Why do you have to twist it around so much?"

"Suppose it was your aged father?"

Jordan sat down. "I'm not going to answer."

"O.K. Suppose you had the choice of having the record of your life's work destroyed, or getting out alive?"

"I don't know."

"Imagine you're eighty."

"I'd want my work saved. I'm going to die sometime anyway."

"Suppose the choice was between personal *immortality* and the preservation of the records of your scientific work?"

"If I had to live on uselessly, I wouldn't."

"I'm giving you a choice between a pleasurable but un-distinguished immortality, or a brief, glorious life."

"I'd take the latter."

"I'd take immortality," said Paul.

"I don't believe you. Look at what you've ac-complished already. Would you throw that away just for immortality?"

"*Just?* Maybe I'm trying to build an immortality through my work, one I wouldn't need if I could live for-ever."

"Bullshit."

"O.K. Let's go back to the first case, where you're in this room with an exact duplicate. Would you flip a coin, fight, or what?"

"I guess we would agree to flip a coin. If we're identical, symmetry requires that we come to the same decision as to what to do."

"Right." Paul sat and sipped at his drink. "I would fight."

"You convinced me that was not the most rational alternative, and now you say you would do it. Why?"

"I couldn't sit by passively and let myself be killed if I lost the toss, and I sure as hell wouldn't agree that we should allow ourselves both to be destroyed. It wouldn't make any difference if the other man was just like me, or nothing like me."

"But if you're both the same you'd have only a fifty-fifty chance of winning, and would probably be badly injured even if you won. You can't seriously say that the less rational action is the one you would take."

Paul leaned back in the teak and black leather rocker. "Michael, you have to realize that a rational choice depends on the situation at the time the choice is made. *Before* a toss of the coin, it's rational to agree to abide by the toss. But there is no enforcement except a reliance on good will. *After* a toss, it's rational for the loser to renege, since his probability of survival, if he goes back on his word, rises from zero to almost one-half. It's like the old nuclear blackmail that used to exist between the U.S. and the Soviet Union. To have a credible deterrent, each side had to believe the other would launch its own missiles if attacked. But once the attack began, there would be no gain in actual retaliation. So the 'credible' deterrent was based on a presumption of irrational response in the crunch.''

Jordan's eyes were closed, and he looked asleep. But he spoke up. ''If we're both identical, I really wouldn't care which of us walked out of the room.''

''There's a basic difference between us, in our concept of personal identity. You regard it as being determined by a complete description of the individual. In my opinion, once there are two replicas, we each become distinct and different individuals, no matter how much we are alike. To me, identity rests on continuity, especially the continuity of conscious experience.''

''So, suppose you undergo hypothermic surgery during which you have no electrical brain activity. Are you a different man when you wake up?''

''No, because there's the physical continuity of the body. If I said I would destroy your body after you went to sleep, say for some experimental reason, and I could put an exact replica in your bed before morning, so that it would be exactly as though you had slept normally all night, would you let me?''

''Sure. If I was convinced you could do it, which is just as impossible as the other example we were discussing.''

''Well, I wouldn't agree to let someone do it to me. Not even if the substitution took place while I had a flat EEG.''

''Why not? By your own hypothesis, there would be no difference in the future course of events, and the new 'you' wouldn't even know that he was a duplicate."

"But suppose I cheated, and *didn't* put the replica in your place. It also wouldn't make any difference to you, since you wouldn't be around. So why does the promise of a replica make it acceptable?"

"Paul, if you were killed instantly, without any warning, it also wouldn't make any difference to you, but you'd still prefer to live. That's a phony argument."

"Not completely. After all, our only experience is of *now*, whenever it is. The past and the future exist only insofar as we remember or anticipate them. But, of course, if I really believed that, then continuity would be an illusion."

Paul finished his Scotch and poured another one. He opened a fresh beer for Jordan, who drank down the rest of his old one quickly. Paul stood and looked out the window. He could see the reflection of the living room, and through it, the dark forms of several boats near the dock. "Michael, I've thought about these things for years, and I don't know the answers. Everything I've said consists of rationalizations. It comes down to this: my feelings are basic, and the reasons are secondary."

"As you said, I guess we have different perceptions about the nature of personal identity. And if we were religious it would be even more complicated, since we would have to argue about the creation and fate of souls, whatever they are." Jordan's speech was slurred and his eyes were closed again. The beer glass dropped from his hand and spilled onto the rug. Skinny, with kinky black hair, Jordan looked like an oversized kid sprawled on the sofa. Paul picked his legs up and put a pillow behind his head, turned out the lights and walked back into his bedroom. He took a sleeping pill and climbed into bed, but his mind was churning. The world is me, and I am the world. The totality exists in my mind. When I die (if I die), the world ceases. Paul pictured his perceptions wiped out. But to imagine something, one has to have a reference point. So, mentally, he eradicated that reference point. But there must be a new one to imagine that, and so on in an infinite regress. Step by step, he backed up, seeing the world, his perceptions of it, his knowledge of *that*, blink out in sequence. So long as my mind exists, it is paradoxical for me to try to imagine my own death. Therefore no man can appreciate the true meaning of death. With each backward mental step, panic closed in on Paul, until he jumped out of bed and stood there sweating. He paced around for a minute to get himself under control, and then got back into bed. He began to doze off, but the part of his mind that watches became alarmed. Paul was wide awake again. He could feel his heart beating heavily as it did when he drank too much. He rolled over on his stomach and embraced his pillow with both arms, feeling the softness beneath his face and chest.

A long time later, he was still awake. He rolled over and got up, walked into the bathroom and urinated. Back in bed, he tried to stay as still as possible. Later on he gave up and began to toss. If I wake before I die, I'll have a chance to say goodbye. If I die before I wake, it's a mistake.

Finally Paul got up and walked to the window. He peeked behind the thick curtains and saw with dismay the horizon outlined against the pre-dawn purple of the sky. He got back in bed and pulled the sheet over his head.

Paul dreamed that another man and he stood outside a door. The man was telling him that the rules were that once they entered the room, Paul could not leave the catwalk *for any reason, under any circumstance.* Paul said he understood. The man opened the door and they went in. It was a very large tile room, dazzlingly white, filled with water over which there was a narrow walkway that ran straight across to the exit at the other side. They started across, and the man turned his head over his shoulder to remind Paul that his *life* depended on not leaving the catwalk. Paul looked down and saw that there was a drop of two meters from the bridge-like walkway to the water below. The man began to speak again, but he seemed to lose his balance, and very slowly, arms waving, toppled off the walkway and into the water. "Help," he cried, "I can't swim." Paul saw a steel ladder at the far side of the large pool. He could swim and could save the man, but he was paralyzed. Is this part of the game? Or was it an accident? Is the man a man, or is he an android?

Paul left the drowning man, walked to the end of the catwalk, *through the door, and into the studio. All around were plaster models, bronze castings, welded steel sculptures, and wooden carvings. He picked up a scooped chisel and a mallet and went over to the carving of the nude woman. He ran his fingers over the textured sur-*

face, brushing away a few lingering fragments of loose wood. Then he began to work on her back, down where the pelvis begins. He rested his left wrist on the wood, placing the chisel in the right position, and tapped just hard enough with the mallet to cut the wood away in a light groove. He continued to work for quite a while, until the curvature at the waist and hip seemed right. He looked at his model, went over and ran his fingers over her waist and hip, and came back to the dark wood. It felt just right, the rough and hard texture just as pleasing in its own way as the soft and pliant feel of real flesh. He stood back and looked at the piece. It was nearly finished and it was beautiful. The model came over to look and spoke to him, leaning against him, her arm on his left shoulder.

The phone rang and Paul sat up in bed. For a few seconds he could still see the studio and the statue superimposed against his room, which was barely lit by the bright sunlight outside. He lifted the receiver. It was Jean.

"Are you coming in today, or should we feed the cells without you?"

·2·

THE NUTHOUSE

ON JUNE 27 Paul signed the voluntary commitment papers. At two o'clock he walked into the clinic, and the orderly locked the door behind them. Paul turned to look around. He had the feeling that the window was unbreakable plastic. The orderly was halfway down the corridor when Paul started after him. Two hundred and fifty dollars a day, and the plaster walls were peeling and the high ceilings left the heating ducts and water pipes exposed. The building smelled and the carpeting was threadbare. Paul felt a sharp twinge, a quick desire to be elsewhere.

The orderly left him in a small office furnished with a desk and filing cabinet. At least I had the sense to bring something to read, he thought. He pulled out *Physical Methods in Ultrastructure Determination* and started to read chapter five. After having read the first paragraph three times without comprehension, he frowned at his

15

lack of concentration and turned to chapter one. The sight of the page disgusted him. He closed the book. Footsteps came down the hall, and Paul got up. They went on past, echoing away in the plaster corridor. He walked over to the window and saw that it could not be opened.

Forty minutes passed. Paul listened to his heart and crossed and uncrossed his legs. He opened the door and heard voices, so he walked down the corridor until he smelled coffee. He opened the door marked "Doctors' Lounge." Immediately the voices ceased, one in mid-laugh. Five heads swung his way, ten eyes devoid of humor. The unfinished sentences hung in the air, the scene a living tableau.

Suddenly two orderlies took him by the arms and began to guide him back to the office. He heard the door lock behind him.

This time he had only a two-minute wait. A stout woman entered and sat behind the desk. She looked at him with her gray eyes and gray hair for a moment. Then she put on her glasses and took out a form.

"Name?"

"Paul Kyteler."

"Address?"

"One fourteen West Island, Cleveland."

"Age?"

"Forty-two."

"Height?"

"One hundred eighty-three centimeters."

"Weight?"

"Ninety-one kilograms."

"Occupation?"

"Chief of the Molecular Biology Division, Eagle Memorial Institute."

"Next of kin?"

"None."

"Anyone we should notify if necessary?"

"Carolyn Peck, my lawyer." He gave the address and phone number.

She put down her pen. "Empty your pockets on the desk." Paul emptied his pockets. She listed the items and said, "Sign." He read the receipt and signed, wishing he had not signed the commitment form that morning.

Then she looked at him again coldly and leaned back in the swivel chair. "You will be Dr. Laughton's patient while you are here."

Paul saw that she was tired and had probably been on duty all night. "Can you tell me what the procedure will be?"

"That's up to Dr. Laughton." Then she left the room, terminating the interview.

The orderly took him to his room, which contained a bed, curtains, a desk, several chairs, and a small dresser. Paul unpacked his suitcase, turned on the TV, and flipped through the afternoon round of soap operas. It was an old-style box model without a projector and without any of the closed circuit technical programing.

He lay down on the bed. The afternoon sun filtered through the curtains and printed their pattern across the floor and rug, and on his legs and the bed. He felt sleepy. The worn and cheap look produced an overwhelming nostalgia. Paul closed his eyes and was in his garret room as a boy, listening to the late afternoon round of shouting from the kids on the block as they raced around outside, engrossed in their non-games. Isn't it perverse, he thought, that it's so easy to go to sleep in the afternoon in the warm sunlight, and so hard at night?

The bell startled him. He sat up in the bed, his heart pounding. It took a moment to recall where he was. He heard voices and feet in the hall, looked at his watch, and guessed that it was dinner time. Standing up, he stretched and started to yawn, but was cut short by the sight of the small TV camera in the upper corner of the room. He stepped toward the door. The camera tracked him with its infrared heat-seeking lens. He opened the door and almost bumped into a young woman in a striped terry cloth robe and slippers as she shuffled past.

He followed the crowd down the corridor, up the stairs, and into the cafeteria. After he got his food, he looked around for someone to join. Most had on their pajamas and robes. He sat down across from a young man with a shaved head who immediately got up and left the room.

Paul heard a woman talking: "So I was in Florida as usual, and Henry hadn't called in a week, so I started drinking again. Then I couldn't sleep, but of course I never can sleep, but I'm scared of taking sleeping pills when I'm drinking. You know, I'm not suicidal, but I'm not sure they believe that, and when I finally realized what had happened, I was in bed with this man I never saw before and I got frightened again. Once I get frightened I can't shake it off, so I came up and signed myself in again. I feel better already and it's so good to have people to talk to, because I hate living in that goddamn empty house alone."

Paul turned around. She was sitting at a table with another woman who was sullenly staring down at her soup and not paying any attention. The speaker was sixty, with heavy makeup on her sun-aged skin, bleached hair, and a loud voice. As he left the room, he saw the orderly counting the dirty forks and knives.

The summer sunset was slow and gentle, but as the room darkened, Paul felt a panic rising. He turned up the volume on the TV and lay back on the bed. But he couldn't pay attention and so he began to pace. The darker it got the worse he felt.

The door opened without a knock and the orderly said, "Medication time." Paul joined the queue at the door marked "Pharmacy" and waited his turn. The woman android checked his name and gave him a small paper cup with a pill in it and a larger cup with some water.

"What is it?"

"It's your medication."

He looked into the cup. It contained one-quarter the amount of flurazepam hydrochloride he was accustomed to. He took it and returned to his room. Somehow he felt better. He still felt better five hours later when he couldn't get to sleep. In fact he felt so much better that things became very clear. He was getting out. He got up, put on his robe and went out of his room. There was a small overhead light on. The nursing station was empty and there was a phone in it. He walked over and punched Carolyn's number. The phone rang for a while, and a female voice said, "Yes, who are you calling?" It was not Carolyn. It must be the inside operator.

"How do I get an outside line?"

"They're all busy right now. Will you hold on for a moment?" Out of force of habit, Paul held on until he realized that at 3 A.M. it was impossible that all the outside lines were tied up. He hung up and turned around just as two male android orderlies pushed through the swinging doors at the end of the corridor, followed by a nurse carrying a syringe. They picked him up and threw him to the floor face down. They flipped up the back of his robe, and the nurse pulled down his pajama bottoms and plunged the syringe into his buttock. In went twenty milliliters of something yellow. My god, he thought, I'm completely cut off from the outside world. The orderlies sat on top of him for five minutes until he became drowsy. Not a word passed among them. Then they led him to his room and locked the door. He lay down on the bed. A huge wave of relief swept over him, then another. He was wallowing in release and a golden glow. It's amazing that the philosophers have missed the one true proof of man's immortality. There is only the present, and it is eternal.

At eleven the next morning he had his first session with Laughton, who was apparently a psychoanalytic resident. He had a face like a puckered marshmallow and hid behind a large meerschaum pipe which he tamped and lit often.

Laughton looked down at the file on the desk top. "Well, Dr. Kyteler. It is *Dr.* Kyteler, is it not?"

"Yes. Ph.D."

"Well, Dr. Kyteler, I notice that there is no referral from an outside physician. Have you been under a physician's care?"

"No, not really. Not for the problem that made me come here."

"Which is?"

"For quite a while I've been having unusual dreams."

"Nightmares?"

"Some are. Some are just strange."

"And how are they strange?"

"They are more like being awake."

"In what way?"

"These dreams have too much detail."

"Our dreams are often detailed."

"These dreams have very realistic sounds, smells, and feelings."

"Yes, go on."

"Also, the events in them sometimes concern things I don't know about."

"We all pick up many cues each day, often unconsciously, and later incorporate them into our dreams."

"In one of my dreams, I was playing the oboe. I've never played an oboe, but I was moving my fingers and reading the music."

"And what was your reaction to that?"

"I didn't know what to make of it. You see, I never

studied music.''

"Did you find the dream disturbing?''

"Not at the time. Except . . .''

"Yes,''

"It's just that I knew I was asleep, and I kept saying to myself, 'What a realistic dream. I'm going to have to remember this when I wake up.' ''

"And you did.''

"Yes.''

"Do you always know you're dreaming during these unusual dreams?''

"No.''

"How often do you have them?''

"Several times a week. Perhaps more. Sometimes I wake up and have a recollection of a dream, but I can't reconstruct it.''

"That's not unusual.''

"I know.''

There was a long silence. Paul kept thinking that Laughton was going to ask him something, but he didn't. They were both leaning back in comfortable chairs, and Laughton's stomach began to growl. He looked at his watch.

Paul asked, "Do you think that my dreams are an indication of something abnormal?''

"We'll just have to try to find out.''

More silence. Paul shifted in his chair. He had been so sure his dreams were pathological. Now, in this room, all he really wanted to do was leave. His dreams didn't seem so bad after all.

Finally Laughton said, "Would you care to tell me why these dreams are bothering you? Do you wake up anxious and afraid?"

"Some are bizarre, but some are very ordinary and have an undreamlike quality. In these, I have memories of things that never happened to me, as though I had another whole life behind me in the dream, as though I were another person altogether."

Laughton was quite interested in this last remark. He began playing with the hairs on the back of his hand. "And what do these persons wish to do? Do they have any particular desires?"

"Nothing unusual."

"What about other characters in your dreams?"

"People I seem to know, but don't, really."

"Well, then, can you tell me why the dreams upset you?"

"I've become afraid to fall asleep. It's as though . . ." Paul became silent.

"As though what?"

"The dreams are so real that I'm sometimes afraid I've become the person I'm dreaming about."

"I see. And that disturbs you."

"Yes."

There was another long silence. Then Laughton asked, "Why?"

"I don't know, exactly."

Laughton looked at his watch. "Well, that's all for today. We can continue tomorrow."

"There's one more thing."

"We can discuss it tomorrow."

As Laughton stood up, Paul thought, you prick, what's your hurry. The scene before him seemed to recede to the end of a long tube. Laughton looked very small, especially his head. He began to fade away, leaving only the echo of his voice. Paul had just realized that the reason the dreams frightened him was that he felt as though, in becoming someone else, his original self would be lost.

After several diffuse sessions with Laughton, Paul knew that he was getting nothing in return. It was almost as if Laughton were not there at all.

On the sixth day he had a visitor. Jean was obviously shocked, and he realized he must look pretty bad. She had come to discuss work, but when she saw him she knew that was out. He told her to get Carolyn in to see him as soon as possible.

An hour after she left, a new man came in. He had a form in his hand. "I'm Dr. Abel, chief of this ward. I hope you're enjoying your stay." Up your ass, thought Paul. "Our preliminary evaluation indicates that ten days will certainly not be sufficient." Paul looked up at the TV camera and realized that there was probably a microphone as well. They wanted to get him to sign something before he saw his attorney. "We would like you to sign a voluntary commitment for an additional sixty days." *Sixty days?* Abel waited but Paul was silent. "I realize that you are busy and that your work is important, but I don't think you realize how precarious your mental state is."

Abel was a short man with a mustache and bloodshot eyes. He took a new tack. "In fact, this is just a convenience, a formality. We can get a judge to sign commitment papers if we think you are a danger to yourself or others."

Paul began to feel panicky. He knew that Abel wanted to bully him into signing. Abel put the form and a pen on the dresser top and sneezed. He turned his head away and managed to spray Paul's pillow.

Paul was diplomatic. "I appreciate this, but since my judgment is a little impaired at the moment, I don't think I should sign without advice. My attorney will be able to advise me, and she will be more objective." Logical, but it didn't stop Abel, who droned on. Finally he left.

Carolyn arrived just before dinner. She was broad boned, with a wide, pretty face and brown eyes, with one blond eyebrow and one light brown eyebrow. Dimples showed in her cheeks when she smiled. Her honey blonde hair was long again, and she was wearing a print dress.

"Your breath smells funny," she said.

"Sorry."

"I know you're nuts, but Dr. Abel had me stop by his office first, and he's *really* nuts. He said you had named me as the responsible party, and wanted me to sign commitment papers for you. I refused to do it. Then he wanted me to talk you into staying on. I said I wouldn't do that either, unless you wanted to, which I gather you don't."

"They can't keep me, can they? Abel said they could, but I think he's lying. I mean in four days I can walk out, can't I?"

"You can walk out now."

"How? What about the papers I signed?"

"I can get them to release you into my custody if you want."

"What does that entail?"

"Not much, really, but ethically speaking, I should keep a close watch on you."

"How do you propose to do that?" Paul thought he knew what she had in mind, but he was playing dumb.

"Well, I've got this spare room, and we'd each have our privacy. Of course, you don't really have to do it. I can get you out of here anyhow."

"Oh." They were sitting on the edge of the bed, not looking at each other. It was so long since they had lived together that the idea was sort of exhilarating.

"You don't have any girl friends who would be jealous, do you?"

"No, not at the present time."

"And after four days you can just move out again."

"O.K."

"O.K. what?"

"O.K. I'll move in for a while."

So Carolyn left the room to make the arrangements, and Paul got dressed and packed. When she came back, they left.

· 3 ·

BRAIN WAVES

WHEN PAUL EXPLAINED what he was going to do, Carolyn asked to come along. She said she had never been inside the Eagle Memorial Hospital-Institute complex and would like to see it. So they drove down together and parked.

"Ever since you started working here I wanted to know who Eagle was."

"Eagle refers to the birds, one of the species killed off by the pesticides."

"I thought Eagle was someone who donated the money."

"The construction grant came from a conservation organization just after the last eagles died. Being predators, at the top of the food chain like us, they accumulated a lot of environmental contaminants. The Institute began during the big ecology scare. It was the same year the Environmental Protection Agency got more money than the Department of Defense."

The Hospital and the Institute were two adjacent buildings of matched design, granite and pink concrete, with vertical, slit-like windows. The Hospital was wide and extensive, with many wings and convolutions so that every patient room had an outside window. By contrast to the Hospital's squat nine stories, the Institute rose straight and square, twenty-three stories high. On the even-numbered floors the two buildings were connected by glass-enclosed walkways.

Paul felt a pang of annoyance when Carolyn smiled at the android parking lot attendant, the android receptionist who checked Paul's I.D. card, and the android elevator operator. They got off at sixteen, at the Psychopharmacology Research Lab.

"Is Dr. Jordan in?"

The android secretary looked up. "He just stepped out for a minute."

They sat down, and ten minutes later Jordan walked in munching on a bag of corn chips. He was wearing a turtleneck shirt and sneakers.

"Hi," he said. "What's up?"

"Michael, this is Carolyn Peck." Jordan started to say hello, but his mouth was full so he just nodded at her. "I want you to lend me a portable EEG unit to record my electroencephalogram while I sleep. Then I want you to analyze the traces."

Jordan's face showed that he was curious, but he didn't ask any questions. "I have just the thing, a cap with no external wires and a remote recording unit. You'll have to sleep in a Faraday cage to keep out stray electromagnetic radiation."

"I'll put copper screening up around my bed. O.K.?"

"O.K."

They went into the lab, and Jordan handed Paul the apparatus. As well as scalp electrodes for the electroencephalogram, the cap had side flaps for the extraocular electrodes and a chin strap for the electromyogram. The whole unit, both pieces, weighed less than eight hundred grams. Paul pretended to throw it to Carolyn, and Jordan's face fell. Then he carried it very carefully down to his car.

After five nights of recording, Paul brought the unit back to Jordan's lab. He was at a lab bench injecting rats and said, "Fine. I'll call you later." When Paul didn't move, Jordan looked up.

"Patience is not one of my attributes," Paul said.

"No one would ever guess." Jordan went back to injecting rats. "If you'll just wait a fucking minute, I'll take a look. I don't want to lose track of what I'm doing." Jordan closed one cage, opened another, and took out the first rat. He picked up a new syringe and continued injecting. "I have to give this intramuscularly because I want a slow sustained release."

"What is it?"

"You wouldn't be interested," said Jordan, knowing that Paul probably would. But he had his day planned out and was annoyed at the interruption. He closed the cage and washed his hands. He took the unit, removed the recording wafer, and put it in the transcriber. As he turned it on, twelve pens jerked to life on the strip chart.

Jordan slowed the chart speed. The paper came through steadily, folding neatly on itself as it fell to the floor. Paul looked closely at the tracings. "You don't know anything about these," said Jordan.

"Right."

Jordan turned up the speed and cut out the damping on the pens. They were now scratching rapidly, occasionally splattering ink droplets off the machine. He switched in the computer feed and punched the EEG analysis program. "Paul, I dug out the MedBank record of your last EEG ten years ago, and it looked almost normal." A smile showed on Jordan's face as he said "almost."

They sat down to wait. Then Jordan said, "This is going to take an hour or so, and I'm not going to waste my time. Lucille, if the machine has a fit, fix it." Jordan's technician looked in from the next lab. She wiped some blood from her hands onto her lab coat. She was busy implanting recording electrodes in the brain of a cat. Jordan went out and Paul sat down to watch the signature of his brain written out in excruciating detail.

"Why did you take so much waking trace if your concern is your dreams?"

"That interval between 12 and 5 A.M. is just the time it takes me to get to sleep."

"I don't think the flurazepam is doing you any good."

"I know it isn't."

Jordan laid out a long section of the chart and pointed to various sections of the parallel traces. He had marked in red ink all over the chart. "This is stage 1 sleep, this is stage 2, and," flipping more leaves, "this is stage 3, and over here you see normal REM sleep." He looked at Paul. "You know, rapid-eye-movement sleep, which in-dicates dreaming." He folded more leaves. "And this is very peculiar. It looks like normal REM sleep, but it isn't. It occurs at about the right time for a long preawakening REM trace. Your eyes are in REM, but there's something funny about it. The fact that it occurs just before awaken-ing could explain why you are so aware of it. People most often remember the dreams that precede awakening. The power spectrum analysis shows slight shifts in the main component frequencies compared with your normal REM."

"Well?"

"Well what?"

"What do you suggest?"

Jordan sat down and began doodling on a pad. "It's not epilepsy. No indication of a tumor. I don't know. We're going to have to be very empirical about this."

"Which means?"

"We are going to have to try things more or less at random and hope it helps. But it could get worse. I don't want you sleeping alone."

"I'm staying with Carolyn."

"Based on guessing, my most reliable method, I'm going to give you a monamine oxidase inhibitor to try a partial suppression of REM sleep. Since the abnormal trace *looks* like REM, maybe it will be differentially suppressed. You know that if we deprived you of all REM sleep, you would become even more irritable than your usual lovely self, and could develop psychotic symptoms."

"If you want to develop psychotic symptoms, just try staying in a mental hospital."

Jordan waved his hand in the air. "Well, don't take any other drugs, starting now. There could be synergistic effects. Keep recording, and if anything bizarre happens, call me, at *any* time." He leaned back and smiled. "Shall I write you a prescription?"

"You'd better. You're the one with the M.D." Just one of their standing jokes.

·4·

COGITO ERGO SUM

"WHAT THE HELL is this sudden interest in machines? I mean you could never sit still and listen for more than ten seconds when I would talk about anything scientific." Paul was deliberately missing the point. It was his way of registering annoyance.

Carolyn slipped the TV dinners out of their wrappers and put them in the oven. "I don't give a damn about machines. I'm talking about people." Paul knew from the fact that her voice was very quiet that she was getting angry. She tried a new approach. "Suppose you started substituting mechanical parts for parts of the body. How many parts would have to be replaced before a man wouldn't be a man anymore?"

"His brain."

"All right. I agree. And so does the law, ever since the Princeton definition of death and murder was adopted."

"And what is the Princeton definition?" Paul was opening a bottle of Chablis.

"Death is legally defined as the irreversible destruction of the cognitive function of the brain. Murder is the intentional destruction of that function. Don't you remember the case where someone injected some chemical into the treasurer of the International Prostitutes Union just before the Senate hearings and destroyed part of her brain? The woman's cardiac and respiratory function was sustained for months until the court decided it was murder and allowed the hospital to let the body die. The court cited the definition proposed by the Princeton Conference specifically in its decision."

Carolyn had become very animated. The oven chimed, and they sat down to eat.

"Since when have you been so interested in science?" Paul repeated.

"It's not science *per se,* but I have to understand the pertinent questions of fact as well as the law. The Princeton definition was also cited when they finally decided the abortion issue. You know." Carolyn got up and turned on the stereo. She put in the Bach-Vivaldi *Concerto for Four Harpsichords.*

"No I don't, but I can guess."

Carolyn reached up to the shelf for a text on constitutional law, opened it, and read from the Supreme Court decision on abortion: "Prior to the initiation of human cognitive function, termination of pregnancy is not to be distinguished from any other medical or surgical procedure, and is therefore a matter to be decided solely by physician and patient without any interference from the state. There are various laws designed for the protection of human life, but we take human life to be identified with the ability for human cognitive function as suggested in the Princeton definition. Thus, as we have held previously, a person in cryogenic storage is alive, despite the temporary suspension of cognitive function, since he or she may be revived at any time. By contrast, the person with irreversible brain damage leading to a permanent loss of cognitive function is dead. It is important to recognize that the designations 'alive' and 'dead' refer to the person as an entity, and not to his parts, organs, or cells.

"Moreover, it is crucial to distinguish between an actual, fully developed ability for cognitive function, such as exists even during suspended animation, and the mere potential to develop this ability over the course of time. Although a fetus has the potential for developing into a person, the same may be said of every cell in the human body which contains a full complement of human genes. If we were to prohibit abortion on the grounds of the potential for development alone, it would be equally required to prohibit all surgery, as this also involves the killing of cells which could, if properly nurtured, become human beings."

Carolyn closed the book. "So it has become the rule to say that the organ which defines a person *is* the brain, because the brain is the seat of cognition."

They finished their shrimp in creole sauce. "Well, I agree that if you transplant a human brain into an android body, the result is a person. O.K.?"

"That may be so, but it avoids the whole issue, which is whether cognitive function can exist in a nonbiological brain."

"So you believe that androids are persons just because they *tell* you they are."

"If it looks like a lion, walks like a lion, and roars like a lion, what is it?" she asked.

"A rabbit."

"Do you know how to catch a rabbit?"

Paul waited for her to tell him. "No, how do you catch a rabbit?"

"You go out into the woods, and you make a noise like a carrot."

"Life depends on cells. Cells are made of proteins, nucleic acids, carbohydrates, lipids . . ."

"Shut up."

Paul looked around at the Danish walnut furniture and the stainless steel and glass coffee table. He looked at Carolyn and could see that she wanted him to make love to her. Although they had separated amicably, he never imagined that they might be intimate again. But she was asking him, and right now she looked very good to him. He stood up and took her hand. At first she drew back, and then, with a nervous laugh, she stood up and followed him to the couch.

As though the ritual had last been enacted yesterday, they undressed, barely looking at one another, folded their clothing neatly on chairs, and stood there awkwardly in their underwear. Then Carolyn walked around the room, turning off all the lights, one by one. Paul used to ask her why she needed total darkness, but her answers had always been evasive. He supposed that light, which stimulated him, probably distracted her. She even closed the front of the stereo cabinet so that the little red "on" light would not produce any illumination.

Paul could tell where she was by the sound of her movement. He heard her lie down on the couch, started over toward it and knocked into the coffee table with his shin. "Shit," he muttered.

"What?"

"Nothing. Just stepped on something."

He found the couch and lay down next to her. He started to take off her brassiere, but she pulled away and removed it and her panties herself. Paul pulled off his undershorts. He reached over to caress her breasts, but she turned away so that she was facing the back of the couch. By this time Paul could see her outline very faintly in the light that leaked into the apartment. He reached around and cupped her breast in his hand. She grasped his wrist very tightly and pushed his hand away. Paul felt his erection subside. He lay on his back, staring at the darkness.

"What's the matter?" she asked.

"Nothing."

"Well, what are you doing just lying there?"

"Carolyn, we used to be married, remember? You know perfectly well what's the matter."

"Well, I'm not going to waste my time lying here if you don't want to get laid."

"I've always been particularly fond of your tenderness at times like this. It's too bad your empathy and compassion are restricted to clients and abstract causes. *I* don't want to waste my time if *you* don't want to get laid."

They continued to lie there. Paul was getting drowsy. He got up to go into the room where they had made up his bed. It's really good that I'm sleepy, he thought. Maybe I won't be up all night.

"Where are you going?"

"To sleep."

"Oh, come on Paul, don't be a bastard. You know what I like. Let's just do it."

He really wanted to say no, but he went back to the couch and lay down on top of her. She was dry, and he couldn't penetrate her. So Carolyn got on top of him, and after a few tries he got into her. They slid around until he was on top. Paul began to move, but she was completely still. Then he slowed.

"What is it?"

That goddamn question again, he thought. "I don't want to come too soon."

"Don't slow down. You know I don't like to string it out."

So Paul moved faster and harder, and within a minute he came. He could tell that Carolyn had come also, as she almost always had when they were married. And, just as then, Paul lay there feeling satiated, but at the same time angry and ashamed of himself. Without coming out he lay there and dozed. When he awoke, his left arm was asleep under her. The stereo wafer was repeating, and Carolyn was drumming on his back with her fingernails. He got up, turned on a lamp, slipped a new recording into the player, and started the shower. After they stepped in, he looked at Carolyn and saw that she had a strange expression on her face. She was staring at him.

"What is it?" he asked.

"How do I know that *you* are human? Maybe you're an android."

"Androids don't screw." Paul began to lather up.

"Yes they do. The men and women androids screw because they were built to. And when they don't, they get as horny as we were tonight."

Carolyn stepped under the spray. She grabbed his penis and began to laugh. "If I cut your balls off, would it make you a robot?"

Paul gave her a playful shove, and she slipped and fell in the tub. He grabbed her arm and caught her, more or less, but not before she had bruised her back. Paul shuddered. How thin a line separates life from death.

As she sat on the edge of the tub drying herself with a towel, Paul watched her breasts shake and thought of their decision not to renew their marriage contract nine years ago. She looked the same as she had when she was twenty-five and they had just met.

"I'm sorry," he said. She looked up at him and there were tears in her eyes. He knew that what they had done this evening had been a mistake, and it seemed she realized it also. It had been difficult to resist, but it brought back old memories that were not too pleasant.

After the shower they made hot chocolate. Carolyn was sitting in her giant panda-bear chair, the big white-and-black fuzzy chair that enfolded her like a palm and fingers. "So, basically you're a modern vitalist," she said.

"What the hell does that mean?"

"I've been reading about the nineteenth-century dispute between the vitalists and the mechanists. You know, 'the essence of life is a vital force'; 'no, creatures are just machines,' and so on. You're saying that if a mind lives in a brain composed of cells it constitutes a person, while if it lives in a factory-wired brain it doesn't."

"No, I'm saying that machines mimic intelligent behavior because that's what they were designed to do, but they *have* no minds. Only cells support life, and life is a prerequisite to mind. How can an android be conscious if it's not even alive?"

"Just as I said. You're a vitalist."

Paul looked down into his cup at the ring of chocolate at the bottom and thought about the tall, blond Norwegian philosopher whose college lectures he had never really understood.

Carolyn was watching him think. "Why do you suppose they made androids?" He looked up. "Elevators can run themselves, cars can park themselves, and restaurants don't need cooks and waiters."

"I guess I don't know. I never thought about it."

"It's because people rebelled against the dehumanization of civilization, the mechanization, the cold impersonality of dealing with machines. People like other people. They like to talk to people. They're gregarious and sociable. But with the revolution in education, no one would take the menial jobs. So finally they couldn't hire anyone at all to work as cashiers or mechanics. Therefore man made androids in his own image."

Paul thought about it. She was probably right.

"Do you know what they call people like you?"

"Who?"

"The androids. You know, they have their own newspapers and magazines, clubs and societies. They call you racist pigs. What do you think about that?" He didn't answer. Carolyn stared down at the table for a few minutes, thinking. Then she got up and walked into her bedroom.

Paul took the plastic bottle of pink tablets out of his briefcase, swallowed two, and walked into the spare room. He stepped into the cage of copper screening that completely surrounded the bed, top, sides and bottom, and closed the wire mesh door after him. He put on the electronic nightcap, switched on the recorder and lay down. It was July 8. For the first time in months he went promptly to sleep.

· 5 ·

PERCHANCE TO REM

THEY WERE RUNNING *through the narrow street. The sun
was so hot and bright that everything seemed faded and
washed out. There were at least a dozen of them, moving
as one. They were armed with crossbows and arrows.
Each arrowhead was filled with an explosive charge.
They stopped the Fiat taxi by pushing it over as it went
by, pulled the android driver out, and cut off his head
with their knives. The streets were strangely empty for
the middle of the day. In the distance there was the wail
of sirens. They ran past an empty sidewalk café and
around the corner. A dog that was standing in the street
disappeared into a courtyard. Two police vans were
parked across the street at the end of the block, and in
front of them stood five android policemen with helmets,
plastic face masks, and large plastic shields.*

*As the runners approached, the police leveled large-
bore shotguns. At thirty meters they fired. The runners
dodged the steel pellet-filled beanbags, all except one who*

was knocked to the street. They separated, some dashing to either sidewalk. In each group, three stood and three dropped to the ground. The police on each side turned to face their nearest assailants. Paul aimed his loaded cross-bow at the space behind the plastic shield of one of the policemen facing the other side of the street, right at his ribs. He pulled the trigger. The arrow sank deep into the cloth and plastic. Two-tenths of a second later there was a muffled explosion and the android crumpled to the street. In fact, all the policemen were down. The runners scrambled around the parked vehicles and split up at the square where four streets merged. Paul ran through an alleyway and into a parallel street.

As he turned right, he faced three android policemen. His crossbow was unloaded. He swung it at the nearest one, but it bounced off the plastic shield. One of them kicked his feet out from under him. He pulled his knife and cut the android's Achilles' tendon. The android went down. Paul grabbed the beanbag gun and turned the pneumatic control from stun to kill. The blast came out with such force that the bag burst, sending the shot through the plastic shield of the second policeman. The sixty pieces of steel tore his chest to shreds. Paul turned to face the third android. The policeman's arms were crossed in the air and were coming down fast. Paul saw the wire in his hands, but was too slow to stop it. It came down and snapped around his throat. Paul punched the android once, vainly, in the chest, but the policeman stepped around him, put his knee in Paul's back, and tightened the wire, strangling him. Paul's head began to swell and his vision blurred. His last thought was: I didn't think androids were capable of killing human beings. Then Paul died.

Paul awakened screaming, his arms flailing against the screening of the Faraday cage. The scream still echoed in his ears as time stopped, and he saw the morning sunlight splashing in through the window. He couldn't move. The door flew open, and Carolyn was standing there in her nightgown, eyes wide and hair mussed. Paul was sure he was dead. He could see and hear, but the sense of death was in every part of his body.

"I said, what happened?"

Paul couldn't speak. He sat there. Carolyn pulled at the door to the cage, but she was pulling at the wrong side of it. "You and your goddamn gadget," she said. She pushed on the other side and tumbled in. "Are you all right?" Carolyn rushed out and he heard her punching the phone. "Dr. Michael Jordan please, and quick."

By the time Jordan got there, Paul was sitting at the table. There was a bowl of cold cereal and milk in front of him, but everytime he tried to lift the spoon, his hand began to shake uncontrollably. He felt as though every nerve in his body were being eaten away. The muscles in his arms and legs were twitching. He could feel that he had lost bladder and bowel control, but it didn't seem to matter.

"Oh, Christ," said Jordan. He put down the case he was carrying, took out a preloaded disposable syringe, and shot it into the vein in Paul's right arm. He released the rubber tourniquet and eased Paul off the chair and onto the floor. He pulled away the pajama top and held the stethoscope against Paul's chest. The amplified sound of Paul's heart filled the room. His mouth was dry and he was not blinking. Jordan went over to the phone and called for an ambulance. Then he went in and picked up the EEG cap and recording unit. Finally he looked at Carolyn. She was frightened.

"Here, let me give you something."

She slapped his hand away and walked into the bedroom. She didn't want to see Paul lying there on the floor.

The ambulance had taken Paul to Eagle Memorial. Later that day he was up and around. He shaved and showered in his lab and got into a cleansuit. He took the elevator to sixteen and walked into Jordan's lab. James Tung, Jordan's postdoctoral fellow, was in the lab with Michael. They turned around when Paul came in.

"Well, we did exactly the opposite of what I had hoped," said Jordan. "We totally supressed normal REM sleep and supplanted it with your abnormal variant. Look." He flipped the folded chart back toward the beginning. "Stages 1, 2 and 3 are all right, but there is none of the usual REM for the first five hours. Then two short periods of this abnormal REM, and then a solid hour of it. This pattern here, where you woke, is very odd. This is where Carolyn took off the cap." The traces jumped and then went flat.

Jordan looked at Paul very closely. "How do you feel now?"

"Hung over, but I'll make it. I still feel like I'm going to crawl out of my skin."

Tung spoke up. "The power spectrum seems to be shifted toward the middle frequencies. It looks like your EEG pattern has been entrained by a mid-frequency driving source. That usually happens only when there is an external sensory input at the driving frequency."

"Couldn't it be that some part of my brain is putting out an abnormal frequency pattern, and forcing the rest of the brain to follow its lead? Isn't that characteristic of epilepsy?"

"If it were one part of your brain, we should get some evidence of localization," said Tung. "No, I think it is some kind of outside influence."

"What do you mean?"

Tung shrugged. "Some outside influence."

"See, an electrical engineer and a mystic," said Jordan. "My opinion is that there is some chemical imbalance that is shifting the oscillators responsible for the EEG potentials. After all, look at what we did to you last night with a drug. It's got to be a diffuse chemical effect." He swung around in his chair and picked up a copy of *Physicians' Desk Reference* and a copy of the *Merck Index*. "I'm going to put you on fifteen milligrams of THC-12."

"Good," said Tung.

Jordan looked at him quizzically. "If you approve, maybe I've made the wrong decision."

"Will you tell me what THC-12 is?" asked Paul.

"It's a chemical derivative of tetrahydrocannabinol, the active component in marijuana. It has a somewhat antagonistic effect to what you took last night."

"Also, it promotes a greater awareness of inner states, to the exclusion of outside influences," said Tung.

Jordan stood up and dumped the books in Tung's hands. "You've got a bachelor's and a Ph.D. When you get your M.D., you can prescribe."

"So you want to put me through the third degree?" quipped Tung.

Jordan grinned and gave him a punch on the shoulder. Tung walked into the adjoining lab. "Paul, maybe he's right. I only know two things for sure. The drug you took last night is no good, and if there are any outside influences, they are not in the electromagnetic spectrum below infrared frequencies. Remember, you were sleeping in a Faraday cage."

· 6 ·

VIRAL TRANSDUCTION AND STRANGE BABIES

PAUL DROVE ACROSS downtown Cleveland to work. Periodically he would let go of the wheel and try to guess how long it would take traffic central to assume control of the car.

He scowled at the android parking attendant and the android elevator operator. The door opened at four and Paul stepped out. He walked into the entrance module to the lab, passed through the shower and drying chambers, put on a cleansuit, and went into the lab proper. Jean and Nadya were there, as usual. They had probably been hard at work since the disgusting hour of eight in the morning. The culture tubes were gently shaking and clinking in the 37°C tank.

"Do we have any new electron micrographs?"

"Of course," replied Jean.

He looked at them. At a magnification of 200,000 diameters, the particles looked like icosahedra in the negatively stained transmission pictures. At ten angstroms resolution from the scanning scope he could see the lattice work of molecules on the surface. He quickly looked to the one angstrom resolution pictures of the isolated DNA strands. He read the base pair sequence in the genes to the splice point where the viral DNA ceased and the newly synthesized DNA had been inserted, and past, back to the remainder of the viral genome. He poured some coffee from the flask on the tripod and walked into his office, poked through the journals, and picked up the latest volume of *Advances in Immunology*. He started reading about antibody synthesis and the control of immune tolerance. Then he went back into the lab, sat down beside Jean, and began pipetting transfers to fresh culture media. Synthetic viruses growing in human kidney cells. My god, if Helen Lane were alive today.

The five third-year medical students were waiting in the seminar room at the end of the hall when Paul walked in. He looked at the photos and names, trying to remember which went with which. Eagle Memorial was one of the teaching hospitals associated with Bratton Medical College, and a few of the students always elected to work at the Institute during their free time block. Paul wondered what they had heard about him through the grapevine. Since he lectured only occasionally, he almost never saw most of the medical students, although he enjoyed the contact.

"Two of you will be working with Dr. Singh in the Biochemical Morphogenesis section." Singh stepped forward from the blackboard and smiled. The door opened. "This is Dr. Otis, whose field is Bioenergetics." Paul saw that they appreciated the fact that Otis was young and very pretty. "She has room for one student. Two of you will be working with me in Genetic Modification. While you are here, you might want to spend some time acquainting yourselves with the work going on in the other eight sections of the Molecular Biology Division as well. We'll split up now and go to the various labs and brief you on what you will be doing for the next six weeks."

As they left the seminar room Paul looked again at the names of the two students who had asked to work with him. Gregory and Olivia Potter, black, twins, and both B.A. with honors from Central High School in the City.

They stopped outside the door to the lab entrance module. "We are working with benign human viruses. However, we observe sterile precautions because we don't want undue exposure to the special genes designed for the patients. Also we don't want to contaminate the tissue and organ cultures with extraneous organisms. Yeasts and *Pseudomonas* are especially troublesome."

They stripped, stepped into the shower, walked through the drying chamber, and put on cleansuits. Paul led them through the first lab and into the second. "This is Dr. Jean Wilson, and Nadya Osgood. Gregory and Olivia Potter. That's Dr. Wilson's office, and this is mine."

Olivia asked, "Is that *Dr.* Osgood?"

"No. Miss."

"Is she . . . uh, where was she born?"

"I really don't know. Why?"

"Olivia wants to know if she's human or android. Not that it really matters, but it's just nice to know."

Paul snapped back, "In this lab there are no androids."

"Is it Institute policy not to use android technicians? Don't you think they would reduce the problem of infection and contamination?" asked Olivia.

Paul shuffled the morning's mail on his desk. "There are androids working in the Institute, but we're not allowed to train them as technicians. Let's drop it, O.K.?"

Gregory poked Olivia in the ribs, raised his eyebrows, and nodded toward Paul. They sat down in the extra chairs.

Paul immediately stood up and stepped to the small blackboard. He drew a hexagon to represent an icosahedron. "The organism we use here is rho-alpha-y, a harmless artificial human symbiont which was first synthesized about twenty years ago. We use it to modify the genetic makeup of patients either to correct inborn errors of metabolism or to cure cancer. We also modify individuals who live on the planetary colonies to allow them to adapt more easily to their environments.

"As you may or may not know, it was the work of Avery, MacLeod, and McCarty in 1944 that proved that DNA was the genetic material. They worked on several different strains of *Pneumococcus* and showed that by transferring DNA from one bacterium to another, you could transfer a genetic trait.

"The method we employ today is derived from the

pioneering work of Zinder and Lederberg on transduction in bacteria. They were able to transfer genes from one strain of *Salmonella* to another by the use of a virus. The virus involved did not destroy the bacterial cell, but reproduced harmlessly each time the bacterial cell divided.

"This early work with bacteria was not immediately applied to higher organisms, such as mammals. Only in the last thirty years have we been really successful in selectively altering the genetic functioning of human cells on a permanent basis. The procedure we use is quite sophisticated. We synthesize copies of the gene the patient needs and make the transducing viruses incorporate this synthetic gene into their own DNA. Next, we grow up large numbers of these enhanced viruses in special human tissue cultures. We add helper viruses which allow the original viruses to multiply, synthesize coat protein, and split open the human culture cells. Then we selectively destroy the helper viruses because we *don't* want this cell destruction to occur when we infect the patient with the transducing virus. When we are successful, the virus becomes, in effect, a cytoplasmic gene, and supplies a missing enzyme, or replaces a defective genetic control mechanism, effecting a cure of the disorder."

Paul led them out into the lab. "We are also involved in various areas of fundamental research. But the work I imagine you will be most interested in is the design of chemotherapeutic agents for the treatment of patients from various hospitals in the area. At the moment we have six such projects going. The most difficult clinical problem we are working on now is the case of a sixty-eight-year old man with metastatic cancer of the prostate gland. We have tried to introduce a DNA sequence to replace the mutated control gene which is responsible for the malignancy. For some reason the modified virus won't grow in the patient's kidney culture cells."

Paul's phone started buzzing. "Jean will show you the protocol, and you can practice transferring culture cells into new growth media." He was walking back to his desk.

"Hello. Kyteler speaking."

"Paul, this is Anna Spaulding. Can we have lunch together today?"

"I'm going to have a baby."

Paul peered at her over his coffee cup. He didn't know whether to offer congratulations or condolences. With the universal acceptance of zero population growth (12 billion was already far too many), having children was hardly the automatic thing it once had been. Yet child rearing was one of the reasons why people sometimes still entered into marriage, and Anna was not married. Even so, with free abortion, and safe, effective chemical contraceptives in wide use, there were very few unintentional pregnancies and births. So Paul put his cup down and said, "That's nice."

They were eating in the faculty dining room at the medical school. The hospital cafeteria was such a horror that Paul almost always avoided it, preferring to eat a sandwich from the vending machines in the basement. So he had been glad to come across town to meet Anna on her own territory.

She was very slight, about 150 centimeters tall, slender, with dark hair and eyes. If you watched her move, she seemed the epitome of femininity. But when she spoke, her hoarse voice created a wholly different impression. In spite of that and her sharp features, Paul liked her personally, enough to have shared a sexual interlude with her the previous year. She had a quick mind, thought not profoundly analytical. At thirty-five, she was the youngest full professor in the Department of Endocrinology.

The waiter brought their apple pie and cheese and placed the desserts on the white tablecloth. "When is it due?"

"It's not due yet because I'm not pregnant yet." Paul wrinkled his brow and had a funny feeling that Anna was going to challenge him with a personal request he wasn't ready to agree to.

"And . . .?"

"And I need your help." She saw his discomfort and laughed. "No, I don't want your sperm, you egotist. I want you to do something for me in your lab."

"What?"

"I want you to grow my fetus *in vitro* until it's ready for implantation in my uterus."

"And who is to be the sperm donor, if I may ask?"

"There isn't going to be one. I'm going to use a nucleus from one of my own skin cells to replace the unfertilized nucleus in my egg cell. I want my child to be my own identical twin."

Paul put down his fork and burped quietly. "Who did you say was an egotist?" He thought, she's a good scientist, but who wants to raise a carbon copy of one's own self?

Anna's face had reddened, and her voice started to shake. "Paul, please do it. I asked B.J. and he turned me down." B.J. Cooke was Chief of Obstetrics and Gynecology at the medical school, and a world authority on *in vitro* fertilization and treatment of infertility. "I went to him because he had done the same thing with two women who kept having miscarriages. They were producing antibodies against their own babies."

"And you have the same condition?"

"No. I don't have any condition. I just want this baby. B.J. said no, not under any circumstances would he pander to the whims of some narcissistic bitch." Her voice broke. "The real reason is, he never forgave me for convincing the rest of the Clinical Research Screening Committee to turn down his proposal for sex reversal surgery in children with homosexual tendencies. He said he wanted to get them before the secondary sex characteristics developed."

"He had a point."

"But *children?* How can a child understand the consequences of such a decision? B.J. and I just fought the whole goddamn thing through again this morning. Besides, he said that wasn't the reason he was turning me down. Of course he wouldn't admit it."

"What did he say was the reason?"

"He said it wouldn't be mentally *healthy* for me and

the child, and that it was morbid and perverse. When I asked him about the other women, he said that there had been a medical indication in those cases. But he's just a damn liar.''

"Suppose I agree. Who will do the surgery? Who's going to remove the egg from your ovary and do the nuclear substitution?''

"Carl and I will do it. You just have to keep the culture alive for a few days.'' Carl was her brother, a vascular surgeon in Houston.

"But he's a thousand miles away! And since when is he an authority in obstetrics and gynecology?''

"Carl will come up here, and he says that there's no trick to it at all. I have the ultraviolet irradiation equipment and micromanipulators to do the nuclear exchange. Paul, I'm asking you because we've been close, and you're my friend.'' Her voice was getting louder. "And if you don't do it, I'm going to bash your goddamn brains in!''

"Shut up and stop glaring at me. I'll do it. I mean, what the hell difference does it make? It's your body. Are you sure you wouldn't like twins?'' In fact Paul felt let down that she was not hinting for a screw. "I'll pay for your lunch, if you'll pay for mine.'' He had switched checks. But Anna had what she wanted and she didn't notice.

· 7 ·

SOME OF MY BEST FRIENDS ARE ROBOTS

PAUL HEARD THE MURMUR of voices as he put the key in Carolyn's door. When he opened it, he realized the living room was filled with strangers. At first they didn't see him, but the young man who was standing in the middle of the room looked up and said, "Hey, cool it!" They all turned to look at him. Men and women were seated around the room, on the couch, on the panda-bear chair, on the hassock, and on the floor. Carolyn was sitting on the floor, papers and books spread out around her.

"Hi, Paul," she said. "Close the door." She stood up. "I won't introduce everyone because you never remember anyone's name anyway. However, I'd like you to meet Angelo, who's been working with me for two months." He shook Paul's hand. He had bushy, brown hair and didn't look too happy. "Angelo has been practicing civil rights law in California. He's going to take the bar exam here next month." Carolyn sat down. "Why don't you join us? This is a legal strategy meeting. Maybe you can help."

Something made Paul uneasy. He felt that Carolyn was humoring him. "No, I'm tired. I'll go into the den and watch the evening news." Paul never watched the news and seldom read the newspapers. He felt it was an unwarranted drain on his mental energy. He walked into the den and closed the door behind him. The hum of voices picked up again, one occasionally rising above the others.

He sat down in the vinyl easy chair and turned on the TV. The wall opposite lit up showing a knot of policemen trying to contain a mob. A cannister snaked through the air trailing tear gas. The announcer's voice was saying ". . . riots in Geneva for the second straight day. There were a dozen women rampaging through the downtown streets, smashing windows and setting fires. Injuries were slight. For the second day in a row, the police failed to capture any of the rioters."

Someone bumped into the cameraman standing behind the police. The camera panned up to show the top of a department store and the blue sky beyond. The scene shifted. A storekeeper was being interviewed. "They broke my window and my display cases. Three women ran around the aisles breaking things and shouting, a mother and her two daughters."

The TV newsman broke in. "How do you know that?"

The storekeeper shrugged. "There was a strong family resemblance."

Outside, a young bystander was already talking. She spoke with a soft French accent. "I saw it all. Everytime the police would grab one, they would all pry her loose. They could not hold on to any of them." She turned to her companion. *"C'était impossible, n'est-ce pas?"*

The scene switched to the studio where the announcer commented: "The police attributed their failure to contain the riot to the fact that there have been no civil disturbances in Switzerland in nearly thirty-five years. Beginning tomorrow . . ."

Paul turned off the TV and the wall went dark. He lay back in the chair and listened to the voices from the living room. Suddenly he jumped up, banging into the oak desk. He had a funny feeling that the strangers in the living room might be androids.

Paul felt betrayed, conspired against. His mind began contracting into darkness. He went over to the cabinet and poured himself a straight Scotch and swallowed it. After a minute, he opened the door and walked into the living room.

This time they did not stop when he came in. They all looked as though they were in their middle twenties. Androids don't grow old; they possess eternal youth, give or take a few repairs. A man with red hair was saying, "I will argue my *own* case. Surely they won't deny me that."

The attorney, Angelo, said, "You refuse to understand! You can't even get into the courtroom except as an exhibit. In the eyes of the law you are a thing, not a person. No, they will never let you speak. You have no choice but to let us try to trick the court into letting you testify on the grounds that we are introducing physical evidence."

The redhead jumped to his feet and started in again, and so did three others. Nothing could be heard through the din. Carolyn picked up a glass bowl and hurled it against the wall. Everyone was quiet.

"Angelo is right. Precedent says that you have no standing in court. That's why we have to bring suit on behalf of a cooperating human."

Several of the androids tried to speak at once. They were angry. "Shut up!" yelled Carolyn. "You are going to decide right now! Do you want us to quit, or do you want us to try? Or maybe you think we won't represent your interests because you can't pay us very much."

The girl at the end of the couch spoke up. "We don't doubt your good intentions, but no one except an android can *possibly* understand how it feels to be treated the way we are. We're *nobodies!* We're free to live our own lives only as long as we don't get in the way of any *human.*" She said "human" with a particular sneer. "Their word is *always* taken over ours. How can you begin to understand what it is like? Martin is right. We have to speak for ourselves in court."

"A presentation in court requires legal training and knowledge as well as commitment. Since androids are denied access to professional training, not to mention licensing, which of you can do the job we can? Isn't the opportunity to do these things part of what we're fighting for?"

Martin with the red hair spoke again. He pointed at the shelf of books on torts, contracts, constitutional law, civil and criminal procedure. He began quietly. "You want to test me? I will bet I can pass any law exam you want to write. I have been reading those books for *ten years* now!"

Carolyn had been one-upped. She looked at Paul. "What do you think about all this?" Paul was leaning against the doorway, his empty glass in his hand. He had been watching with juvenile fascination a scene as devastating in its own way as his crazy dreams. "What do you think?" repeated Carolyn.

Paul sat down on the floor. He was looking back and forth from face to face. The kaleidoscope of emotions, of expressions, the intensity of feeling hammered against his mind.

"Paul, Terry and Desmond want to get married. They can't get a license." She pointed to a couple sitting together on the rug. "I *can* go to court on Desmond's behalf because he's human. I can attempt to argue that laws prohibiting intermarriage are invalid."

So Desmond is not an android. Good fellow, Desmond.

"Joshua was named sole beneficiary in the will of the man who had him built to specification. That man regarded Josh as his real son. The man's sister is suing to break the will. I have no grounds to challenge her action because in the eyes of the law, Josh is not a person, he's a thing.

"Elisabeth had a friend and companion named Susan." Paul looked at Elisabeth. She was at least fifty and undoubtedly human. Funny he hadn't noticed her before. "Susan was killed by a drunk driver while they were walking along a country road near Elisabeth's house. She tried to get the District Attorney to press manslaughter charges. He refused on the grounds that one cannot kill a machine and advised her to sue for damages. But Susan was her friend, and one does not make friends with a *thing*.

"Paul, do you know what they do to an android who is *accused* of a criminal act? There is no arraignment, no trial. He's sent back for 'factory readjustment.' Did you know that their personalities can be completely changed by that 'readjustment?' Years of memory can be totally lost, recollections of friends wiped out. There is no 'due process' for androids, no 'civil rights,' certainly no *habeas corpus*. Do you know about the Dred Scott decision in 1857? It said that runaway slaves were property and had to be returned to their masters even if they had escaped to the North. That's about where we stand today.

"Let me read you what Justice Fender of the Ohio Supreme Court said." She picked up an open book. " 'A suit on behalf of a machine is no more valid than a suit against God for damages resulting from a natural disaster. To take up the time of the courts with such frivolous matters is inexcusable.' " She slammed the book shut.

"What do you think, Paul? Can't a smart bastard like you think of something that will help us? We are only bucking every precedent that the state and federal courts have established over the last thirty years."

Paul was still looking from face to face. He began to think wild thoughts. I worship at the altar of the trinity: DNA, RNA, and protein. What the fuck are they all looking at *me* for? You would think *I* had something to do with *them!*

Paul had been staying with Carolyn for six weeks. He had moved his typewriter and books from his house on the lake, and had settled in. He was still sleeping in the cage, and Jordan was still reading his EEG, but the THC-12 had eliminated all apparent abnormality. Carolyn and Paul had both been lonely recently, and each benefited from the presence of the other so long as they kept their relationship fraternal. The only awkwardness occurred when her android friends came over to argue about their civil rights activities. Paul sat in on all the sessions when he was at home, watching and listening intently, but never saying anything. Carolyn was deeply involved in the android underground and subculture, and her total identification with the cause had obsessed her.

Her law partners shared her ideals, in an intellectual sort of way, and were underwriting her civil rights activities, but they did not want to be directly involved and have dissident androids mingling in their offices with corporate executives, government officials, and other posh clients. They salved their consciences, with some justification, by the argument that but for their regular business, Carolyn would not have the resources and time to pursue the cause. Besides, once a case came to court, it would all be out in the open and the shitstorm would begin.

Carolyn had decided to press the case of Terry and Desmond, who wanted to get married. Paul was struck with the irony of such a situation at a time when marriage between humans was on the decline. She was constantly occupied preparing her trial brief, researching precedents, looking for ways to manipulate the rules of evidence, and reading previous decisions of the federal district judge who, hopefully, would hear the case.

One evening Terry and Desmond came over for dinner and a discussion of their case. They were sitting around the oiled walnut table eating Chicken Kiev and Eggplant Provençal that Carolyn had taken great pains to prepare, when Paul found himself staring at Terry. He couldn't remember having seen an android *eat* before. He wanted to ask a question, but it wouldn't come out. Finally Carolyn turned to him and asked, "Don't you like the eggplant? You used to."

"Carolyn, can I talk to you for a minute?" They stepped into the kitchen, and Paul asked his question. He felt his ears burn when Carolyn started laughing. She didn't answer him, but led him back to the table.

"Paul wants to know how it is that you're eating food."

"Why Dr. Kyteler, is this the first time you've ever seen an android eat?"

"I don't know. I can't seem to remember."

Terry's cheeks had begun to flush. She was apparently embarrassed too. "We all eat. We *have* to eat." Paul's question had turned a mundane matter into a discussion of intimacies.

"But what happens to the food?" Paul imagined a plastic sack instead of a stomach that Terry would dump into the toilet later when she was alone. He assumed androids worked on batteries and plugged themselves in to recharge at night.

"I digest it. I don't need vitamins and proteins, but I get my energy by burning organic matter just the same as you. Why do you think I breathe?"

Paul could see Terry's breasts rise and fall as she breathed. Somehow he hadn't noticed before. Apparently she used atmospheric oxygen to oxidize food in a manner which mimicked human respiration. She probably had intestines and an anus as well.

"I'm sorry." Paul sat down.

"That's all right." Terry began fidgeting with her food. She was still ill at ease.

Paul also wasn't eating. Without looking up he said, "Terry, do you have a heart?"

"Of course."

"Can I listen to it?"

"If you like."

Paul got up and walked around the table. He bent down and pressed his ear against her. She was warm. He could hear what sounded to him just like a human heart and breathing noises. Suddenly Paul felt awkward with his face in Terry's chest. He stood up.

"What does it do?"

"It circulates high energy compounds and electrolytes to my muscles and brain. I'm just a little bundle of chemical transducers." She gave a nervous laugh.

Paul could smell her perfume. He looked at Desmond, who wanted to say something but couldn't decide what. Paul lifted Terry to her feet and embraced her. He could feel her breasts deform as they touched him. He could feel her hips against his. He leaned down and kissed her and could taste the food on her lips. He could certainly feel her breathing fast. She still had her fork in her hand.

"Dr. Kyteler, I wish you wouldn't do that. Terry is my fiancée."

"If I'm going to give the bride away, I'd like to get to know her a little better." Everyone laughed, and the mood of tension relaxed. How odd, thought Paul, that all this has escaped my attention. "Besides, my name is Paul."

The legal talk had been suppressed for the evening. After dinner they sat around in the living room. Terry asked, "Do you have the latest Nonesuch release of the four Mozart horn concerti?"

"No," answered Carolyn, "but I have another recording of them."

"Well, you'll have to get it, because Desmond is the soloist. The Cleveland Orchestra decided he was just as good as any outside soloist they could get."

"You're a musician," Paul stated superfluously. He was feeling a little silly from the strange dinner and the wine.

"Yes. French horn."

"*First* French horn," added Terry. "And he also plays piano."

"What do you do, Terry?" Paul realized as he was speaking that it was probably a mistake, but it was too late.

Terry wasn't smiling, but she held her chin up. "I'm a waitress at McDonald's across from the Greyhound bus station."

There was a long silence.

"But someday I'll be a concert pianist." She turned to Carolyn. "It's safe here, isn't it?"

"Do you have to ask after everything that's gone on in this apartment? I have gadgets all over to warn me if there are any electronic bugs."

Terry got up and went over to the harpsichord on the far side of the room. She sat down and played several selections from J.S. Bach's *Well-Tempered Clavier* and from the *Two and Three Part Inventions*. She played well. When she had finished, she walked over to Desmond and kissed him. "Desmond is teaching me."

"She's the quickest study I ever saw. She even composes. Two years ago she couldn't play a note."

Carolyn broke in. "You know, Paul, that Desmond could get a year in jail and a five-thousand-dollar fine for teaching Terry." It was a sobering thought. Paul could feel a sense of fury and frustration that this young couple had to sneak around to make love and music in secrecy.

· 8 ·

POOR SPRAGUE

PAUL'S LAB RAN almost effortlessly. Although half of his time was devoted to administrative work concerning his section and the others that constituted the Molecular Biology Division, he managed to spend at least four hours a day working in the lab with his own hands. The lab was not merely a service outlet for the clinical departments at the hospital and the medical school. Although it had generally been accepted, in theory, that viruses must have come from the DNA (or RNA) and protein of their original host organisms, Paul had been the first to show experimentally that they could originate as fragmentation products of cells. By the use of chemical mutagens, he had shown how to produce viruses at will. This had finally unified the theory of carcinogenesis, since it had long been a puzzle why radiation and chemical mutagens, as well as viruses, could cause cancer in animals and humans, and why the same agents could also be used in

71

treatment.

Paul's pocket page buzzed. He walked over to the wall phone, punched the operator, and gave his name. She put him through. He could hear muffled voices as though someone had his hand over the phone. Then a voice said, "Paul?" It was Wendell Guth.

"Hi Wendell."

"Paul, how's your time this afternoon?" Then the voice receded from the phone. "No, I said we have to send in all five copies with the grant application. You'll have to make two more for our files and one for the director's office." A feminine voice commented inaudibly, and Paul heard a door close. "Sorry, Paul. Can you come over here this afternoon?"

"Not easily. We're going to do a readout on the organ culture for your prostatic carcinoma patient. They're waiting for me upstairs right now."

"Paul, maybe it doesn't matter. If you don't mind, I'd appreciate it if you could come over here instead."

"You're the doctor. If you want me, I'll come."

"Thanks, Paul."

Wendell Guth was Associate Professor of Medicine at the med school, and the patient was his responsibility. Paul got on the crosstown university shuttle bus, and in fifteen minutes he walked through the glass doors of the small teaching hospital immediately adjacent to the medical school building. At the third floor he got off and went to Guth's office. Guth was a plump man in his fifties with a bald forehead, gray hair, and large, bushy, gray eyebrows that curled up at the ends and gave him the look of a fat elf. In his office was Leo Morris from Radiology. On the illuminated light boxes on the wall were various x-rays and ultrasonic scans, and on the desk was a computer printout of blood chemistry and gas chromatography analysis dated August 17, which it was. On the top was the name Elmer Sprague, the cancer patient.

"Paul, our man is dying."

"Why?"

"He came out of remission. As you know, we used antibodies to the tumor toxohormones. That should have stopped the cancer from spreading and provided symptomatic relief. For some reason it didn't work. Last night the patient checked back in with severe bone pain, and it was spreading out of control." Guth was pointing out various tumors on the x-rays and on the ultrasonic visualizations. "There's no doubt he's terminal. Leo wants to try neutron irradiation, but I wanted to talk to you first." He paused and started pacing in front of his desk. "Why the hell won't the virus work?"

Paul didn't answer the question. "Can we see the patient?"

Guth nodded. They walked down the hall and pushed open the extra wide door. An emaciated man lay in the bed, a drainage tube in his nose, an intravenous tube connected to his arm, and a bladder catheter emptying urine into a plastic bag at the foot of the bed. His eyes were half closed. Paul looked at the chart. He was on morphine.

They stepped out into the hall. "If you think there is an alternative to radiotherapy, just tell me," said Morris.

"But frankly, if I don't get him now, I don't think he can survive the radiation dosage itself." They went back to Guth's office.

"How long will he last?" asked Paul.

"I can't say. He could push off at any time."

They sat there, quiet and depressed. Finally Paul said, "Let me call my lab." He didn't expect to find out anything useful, but he wanted to break the silence. He punched the number, and when Jean got on the phone she was excited.

"Paul, we found out what was wrong with the transducing virus we made. Nothing!"

"What? What do you mean?"

"Well, we couldn't harvest any virus from Sprague's kidney cultures, so yesterday we prepared a batch of transducing virus with tritiated thymidine. We innoculated some culture cells and then fractionated them. There were no radioactive small nucleotides, so the synthetic DNA is intact. Then we checked out the helper virus, and there's no problem with it either. When we found out that the stock viruses without the new DNA wouldn't grow either, we did an interferon assay. The cells are producing it like mad."

"You mean it's just interferon preventing synthesis of viral protein?"

"I'd bet on it. We can take a second culture from the patient to see if his cells are all producing interferon or if it happened after they were transferred to the lab."

"There's no time. He's dying."

"Oh. Is that why you went over?"

"Yes. I'm with Wendell and Leo Morris now. What I want you to do is to take the gene we synthesized and start growing it up on human kidney culture #7. In a few hours we can have enough transducing virus to use."

"Paul, I'm sorry, but we used up the last of the DNA prep yesterday."

"What about the chromatography columns?"

"We dismantled them and cleaned them up. The one we used yesterday was hot, and I threw it out."

"O.K. It just means a few hours delay." Paul turned to Guth, who had been listening on the open speaker. "Do we have enough time? I can have the transducing virus for you tomorrow."

"Probably. But I can't give any guarantees."

Paul turned back to the phone. "Jean, we have an all-night job. I'll leave here right away. You and Nadya begin to set it up."

"Nadya is in New Orleans. Her vacation began today. Don't you remember?"

Damn, thought Paul. "How about Greg and Olivia?"

"They left ten minutes ago."

"Well, call them and tell them to get their asses back to the lab quick. I'll be there in fifteen minutes."

When Paul got into his lab, he checked the base sequence in the *Atlas of Human Gene Sequences*. Then he layered the matrix bound enzymes (sixteen different exonuclease-dinucleotide-resin varieties) in the chromatography column in the correct order to snythesize the polynucleotide strand. In between each layer he placed a layer of matrix bound cleavage enzyme to remove the blocking group from the end of the polynucleotide after each step in the polymerization. The finished first strand would then serve as a template for the construction of its complementary partner in the double helix. He checked to make sure they had some freeze-dried virus, and set up the culture tubes. When the gene was finished and purified, it would take another six hours to grow up the viruses so that they would incorporate it.

By this time Greg and Olivia were back at work. Olivia started the buffer with the blocked mononucleotides flowing through the column to pack it and stabilize the pH.

Paul looked out the window at the rush hour traffic still in progress. It won't get dark until after eight, he thought. At 11:30 he opened his briefcase and took out one of his THC tablets. No sense taking chances.

At 3 A.M. they came off the synthesis column. By 4:30 they had run through the purification gel. At 5:00 the second strand had been polymerized onto the first. By 7 A.M. they were ready to innoculate the cultures. The phone in Paul's office buzzed. He picked it up with his left hand, his right hand holding a half-filled five-milliliter pipet.

"Paul, I'm sorry." It was Guth's voice. "Sprague is dead."

He shut off the shakers and the magnetic stirrers and the lights, and they all left. As he drove, Paul found a children's nonsense poem rattling around in his head:

It was a dark and sunny morning
On a hot and frigid night
When two dead boys came out to fight.
They faced each other, back to back,

Drew their swords and shot each other.
One deaf policeman heard the noise
And came to rescue the two dead boys.

On his way home Paul passed an all-night bar he had often seen but had never been in. He felt rotten, so he drove his car around the block, parked it on the street, and went in. In contrast to the bright sun outside, the bar was dimly lit. He sat down on a stool and ordered a Scotch on the rocks.

As his eyes became accustomed to the darkness, he saw a very pretty young woman sitting at one of the tables sipping at a beer and periodically looking at her watch. Paul glanced at her from time to time as he drank another Scotch. Once, she looked up and saw him and gave him a nervous smile. She looked away, and then back, and smiled more genuinely. He picked up his drink and walked over to her table.

"May I sit down?" She gestured at a chair. "Are you waiting for someone?" he asked.

"It doesn't look that way. I mean, I thought I was, but I guess I'm not." She drank some more beer and smiled at Paul again.

Paul put his hand on her knee. After a couple of minutes she took hold of it and pulled it up between her legs. Her panties were moist. He wondered if she were a whore, and he thought she might be, but she had more the look of a university student. He imagined that she had been stood up and had been sitting here for quite a while. He didn't like the idea of taking advantage of the situation, but he was not too sober, and besides, there was something about the way she spoke and held herself and about her smile that Paul found unusually attractive. He began to stroke her softly. She caught her breath and closed her eyes.

"Would you like to go up to my place? It's really very close."

Paul nodded. "What's your name?"

"Sarah. What's yours?"

"Paul."

They got up. He paid for the drinks, and she took him by the hand and led him out the back of the bar. Just before they went out he pulled her to him and kissed her. She clung to his neck and pressed her hips against his. They went out the back, across the street and up the front steps of an apartment building. Her place was on the second floor. She unlocked the door and they went in. There was a combination living-dining room with a small kitchen off it and a bedroom in back, with no doors separating them. It was neat and cheerful, but the furnishings were cheap.

Sarah pulled back the covers on one of the two beds and went into the bathroom. Paul undressed and climbed into bed. It was extremely soft, and he sank down into it. It felt comfortable, but he knew that if he slept on it his back would hurt. She came out of the bathroom nude and walked to the bed. She smiled again, and Paul thought that she was the sexiest thing he had seen outside of his dreams. The morning light was coming in through the drawn curtains and cast only the softest shadows. She had curly hair, dyed a fashionable pink, high cheekbones, and absolutely precise proportions. She lifted the covers and saw his erection.

"Oh, my, did I do that to you?" She lay down next to him, and they put their arms around each other. He closed his eyes and let her fragrance surround him. Her skin was so soft that he kept stroking her shoulders with his fingertips.

They heard the sound of a key in the door, and both jumped.

"Quick. You'd better go into the bathroom."

"Hell I will," said Paul.

She shrugged, indicating that she didn't really care. She got up and went into the living room. There was the sound of another female voice. Sarah came back in, still naked.

"It's all right. It's only my roommate. She won't stay long, but she has to get some things."

Paul got up and put on his clothes. He was annoyed at the interruption, but he smiled at Sarah, knowing that they would resume in a few minutes. He walked out into the living room. Sarah's roommate and Paul recognized each other instantly. She was one of the androids who regularly attended the sessions at Carolyn's apartment. She looked from Paul to Sarah, and back, an expression of concern on her face. It was obviously one of the last things she would have expected.

Then the full significance of the situation overtook him. If Sarah's roommate was an android, Sarah was too. His stomach began to churn. He pulled the door open and ran down the stairs and the outside steps. He walked to his car, set it on automatic, and programmed it to take him home.

· 9 ·

CLONES

PAUL WAS DEPRESSED the entire following week. He tried to analyze his feelings. Technically Sprague had not been his patient. He had never talked to the man and had never seen him until that last night. Still, he felt partly responsible, or perhaps just sad. If only Guth could have given him a few days to work with. But there had been no way.

He attended the post-mortem presentation by the pathology resident. Acute bronchial pneumonia leading to pulmonary edema. Congestive heart failure. Kidney failure. Forty-odd metastases in the bones and lungs. Guth was subdued but businesslike. By contrast, Leo Morris seemed sullen and resentful. Radiotherapy, the great shining hope of the early days, was rarely used now.

Paul watched the medical students taking careful note of the case history, watching the color slides prepared by Pathology, and asking questions. When it broke up he started to leave, but he saw René Marchant and walked over to him. René had his tennis racket and was heading out the door. "Hey!" called out Paul. "Going somewhere?" René turned around and grinned widely, as usual. He slapped Paul on the arm.

"Paul! I haven't seen you on the courts for a year." Paul and René used to play three times a week during the warm weather. René was a thoracic surgeon, but Paul's contact with him was purely social. He not only played tennis, he played piano, sang, told dirty jokes, and was never unhappy. He was almost the exact opposite of Paul, who was brooding, introspective, and chronically anxious. So Paul liked him. In fact, he envied René.

"Have you had lunch?"

"No," said Paul.

"Come watch me play a set and you can eat with me and my daughter."

They walked across the street to the municipal park with the swimming pool and tennis courts and the children's zoo. There, dressed in white, was a young woman who looked as though she might have been René's little sister rather than his daughter. "She lives in Bonn with her mother, you know."

"No, I didn't know you had any children."

"It happens in the best of families. Lotte, this is Paul, my friend."

Paul watched them play in the noon sunshine. He was sitting on a park bench and the sun was filtering between the leaves as they moved in the summer air. Occasionally the wind would make them toss and shake. It felt good in his hair and on his face. Paul took his shirt and shoes and socks off. He heard the voices of children romping with the lambs and rabbits and little monkeys in the children's zoo. He couldn't really see in, but he imagined he could. I was once a child, a long time ago. No, I am what I am at this moment. The world is recreated each instant and the past is an illusion. He opened his wallet and took out the picture of his parents taken on their thirtieth wedding anniversary when he was eleven. He often wondered how different they had been from what he was. Easygoing, phlegmatic, married to each other for life. They were both dead, and in a way Paul felt he had never known them. They had been so quiet. I am your only child. You live on in me, and I remember you no better than if you were two lovely characters in a film. He closed his eyes and lay down on the bench.

He was next aware of Lotte tickling the soles of his feet. "Let's get some hot dogs and ice cream and have a picnic on the grass." She spoke with a slight, ill-defined European accent. Both she and René were dripping with sweat. They bought the food at the refreshment stand in the children's zoo and sat down at one of the picnic tables.

"Paul, you'll never guess what I'm going to get to do." René was beaming.

"You're right. I'll never guess. What are you going to do?"

"I have a patient with a severe myocardial infarction. I am going to do a regular old-fashioned heart transplant to fix him up!"

At that moment, Paul couldn't imagine anything he wanted less to hear about. He took a drink of his root beer. René went on. "Actually, it's a stroke of good fortune." An odd way to feel about such a thing, thought Paul, but I suppose optimism is good in a surgeon.

"Why are you going to open that bag of worms, with perfectly good artificial hearts available? I mean, to start tampering with the immune response system for no reason, just to prevent graft rejection. And you can grow a new heart in compatible culture in two years. I don't understand what you could mean by good fortune."

René suppressed his smile, with difficulty. "Ah, but with a master like me, Paul, those problems never arise." He broke into laughter, and so did Lotte. Their eyes twinkled in unison. Paul shrugged as if to say you can let me in on it if you want. It was making him feel very morbid.

"Have you no curiosity, Paul?" René leaned on his arms across the picnic table and thrust his face near Paul's. When he saw that Paul was going to remain silent, he said, "I'll tell you anyway. There will be no immune rejection because the man is a Clone Thirteen!"

Paul wrinkled his brow. What was a Clone Thirteen? And what did clones have to do with people? Of course, all laboratory animals were reared by cloning. They were ideal subjects for biological experimentation due to the complete genetic identity of the members of any given clone. And a set of identical twins could be considered a human clone with two members.

Then he suddenly recalled his project with Anna. Just

as was the case with laboratory animals, any cell from a person can give rise to a fetus by donating its nucleus to replace the unfertilized nucleus of an egg cell. The unfertilized human egg nucleus has twenty-three chromosomes, and in conjunction with a sperm during fertilization acquires the normal diploid complement of forty-six chromosomes. But the somatic, or body cell, nucleus already has the full forty-six, and when introduced into the mature egg, embryonic development is initiated. Since the genes in the nucleus are the repository of the hereditary information, a baby produced in this way would be an identical twin to the donor of the nucleus.

In Anna's case, she wanted to be her own donor. However, there had been some notorious cases where women had requested cell nuclei from some particular man or woman, some outstanding figure in the arts or sciences or in politics. Organ cultures of these individuals lived on even after the death of the original donor, thus providing a perpetual reservoir of transplantable nuclei. It was one of those fascinating oddities found in genetics texts and seldom heard of again.

René had been speaking, but Paul had not been listening. "Paul, did you know that?"

"What?"

"Every time a clone member dies, his entire body is preserved by freezing. There is a central body bank in Amsterdam with bodies from each clone. So I take the heart from another Clone Thirteen body and transplant it. *Voilà!* No immune rejection. Absolute compatibility." René looked so pleased that you would think he had been responsible for the whole idea in the first place.

"René, how many human clones are there?"

"Ah. Two dozen. Three dozen. I don't know."

"And how many members of each clone?"

"Who can tell?"

René and Lotte tightened their rackets in the presses and ran off through the warm summer air, across the grass and between the trees. They ran across the street to the medical school to shower and change. A strange idea came to Paul. Suppose a man and a woman from the same clone had a child? But then he realized the folly of his imagination. All members of a clone would be of the same sex as the donor: XX for women, XY for men. Still, if one wanted, he could microsurgically remove a Y chromosome and replace it with a second X so that one could have a nearly identical mate. "Learn to love me, and you will love yourself." But Paul didn't greatly like the idea of a female counterpart of himself. He felt a latent incest taboo. Besides, differences make life interesting.

He took the helicopter back to Eagle Memorial and looked out over Lake Erie. He remembered the pictures and descriptions of the lake in the old days, before it had been brought back from the grave.

·10·

REALIZATION

JORDAN TOOK PAUL'S PULSE and blood pressure, examined his retina with an ophthalmoscope, tested his reflexes and his tactile discrimination. "O.K. Paul, let's not knock a good thing."

"A complete cure. At last," mocked Paul.

Jordan screwed up his face. "Let's just say it's temporarily under control. If you don't mind, I'd like my EEG back. Let's see." He pretended to make a calculation. "The rental fee is . . . sixty-two thousand dollars."

"That must be what the unit cost you."

"Exactly."

"So you don't want to read any more traces?"

"I can't afford the time. I haven't been able to do anything else." Paul knew that after the first week the recordings had been processed entirely by computer. "No, unless you develop a recurrence of symptoms, we'll let it ride. Your blood pressure is slightly down, but that won't hurt. And now I'm off to see a skin flick."

Paul thought he was kidding since it was the middle of the day, but the newspaper on Jordan's desk was open to the movie and theater page. Sure enough, an item was circled: *"The Courageous Cunt.* Call for times." Paul closed the paper. The headline on page one said, "Mass Suicide in Kyoto." He read on. "Reuters. Sept. 1—The Kyoto city government has reported that at least ten persons jumped to their death at 8:30 P.M. at widely scattered places throughout the city. The Prime Minister was unavailable for comment, but the Minister of Tourism speculated that it might be an attempt to embarrass the Japanese Government on the eve of the International Trade Fair [See story on p. 3]."

Paul turned to page three. "Kyoto Suicides. This bizarre event may be the latest in the outbreaks of mass hysteria which began over a year ago. However, it was the first such incident in which there was loss of life. Last month's women's riot in Geneva seemed to be a ritualistic revival of the university riots of last century. The most serious previous disturbance was the street fighting in Milan where a number of police androids were destroyed with bows and arrows."

The article went on, but Paul read this last sentence over and over. The room seemed to grow very pale. The cheerful walls faded to a pastel hue. He felt drops of sweat falling from his armpits into his shirt.

He punched for the elevator. It was on two and coming up. He pushed open the stairwell door and started down from sixteen. He felt faint and almost fell. He left the stairwell at fifteen and punched the button again. The elevator door swung open. Paul looked at the elevator operator, who looked back uneasily. On four he got out. He went into the men's room and sat on the floor, put his hands in his stomach and doubled over. Little flashes of light were popping in his head. After a few minutes, he got to his knees, wet a paper towel, and pressed it to his forehead. He felt better and stood up. Immediately he felt faint again. He staggered out into the hall, past the emergency shower, and ripped open the wall-mounted first aid kit. He crushed a gauze-covered ammonia capsule and inhaled. It almost blew the top of his head off. He leaned against the wall, sniffing ammonia from time to time.

Finally he walked into his lab. He was drenched with sweat, but the shower refreshed him. In a dry cleansuit he walked into his office. Jean wanted to talk, but he waved her off. He sat down at his console and punched "NEWSPAPERS/NEW YORK TIMES /JULY 9," the day after his nightmare. The front page appeared with a headline about a meeting of the Council of Ministers of the African Economic Community. He punched for the index and scanned it until he came to the title, "Riot in Milan." He punched the index code and held down the hardcopy button. In thirty seconds out came a printed copy of the story complete with color photographs. One of them looked much too familiar. He read the article, then leaned back in his chair. He looked up at the bulletin board over his desk and the notice that said "International Union of Virology. Meeting 13-15 September, Naples. Call for Abstracts." It was dated April 4 and said the deadline for submission of abstracts was June 21.

Paul had decided not to go this year because of Federation Meeting and Biophysical Society and the grant review panels.

He punched the operator. "Operator, I want to call Naples, Italy, person to person to Professor Manuel Cardoza at the International Laboratory of Genetics and Biophysics. I don't know the number." The operator got someone on the line who said to call the Marine Biological Laboratory and gave a number and extension. In two minutes Cardoza was on the phone.

"Hello, Manny?" Cardoza hated American nicknames.

"Paul! Are you here?"

"No, I'm calling from Cleveland. How have you been?"

"Fine. My son has just passed his Ph.D. comprehensive examination and has started his dissertation."

"In philosophy?"

"No, he switched to classical literature."

"He must be twenty by this time."

"Twenty-one."

"And your wife?"

"Fine. Actually, not too well. It's not serious, but she's working only half-time now. Tell me, when will we see you again?"

"That's what I'm calling about. I want you to get me on the program at the September meeting."

"You're welcome to come, but the deadline for abstracts was June. You didn't send one in, did you? I don't remember seeing one from you."

"No, I didn't, but I have just got some new and dramatic results." That was a lie, but Paul could always dig up something he hadn't presented before.

"I'm sorry, Paul, but the schedule has been arranged for some time. You know how it is."

"Manny, look, if you're the program chairman, you can slip me in."

"I don't put the program together by myself. The program committee . . ."

"Manuel, do you remember when you forgot to confirm your hotel reservation in Chicago two years ago?"

There was a silence for a few moments. "The abstracts and schedule have already been printed and mailed out."

"I don't care if it isn't on the printed program. I just want to be scheduled."

"Well, the last fifteen-minute papers are usually set for 5:15, but I did put a few at 5:30 on the fourteenth. I can add yours on to the end of one of the other sessions at that time. But you know they are usually running late by then and attendance is off."

"That's all right. It will be fine. Thanks. I won't forget it."

Paul hung up. Well, now that I'm on the program, my grant will pick up the travel expenses. Who the hell am I kidding? He realized that the reason he had felt the necessity of an excuse to go to Italy was that he couldn't let himself accept as fact what he knew to be true. But if I realize that about myself, why do I need a subterfuge? I *am* myself, and whatever I realize about myself cannot be hidden from me. Paul couldn't explain it. It was as though more than one individual was struggling to control his actions, and the device of the meeting made going acceptable to all parties.

Paul was going to fly into Rome on September 11. He wanted a day to let his biological clock start to adjust to the time change, so that he would be alert at the meeting. Somehow he had almost blocked Milan out of his mind. He had, in fact, some very interesting preliminary results to report on a new viral coat protein that he had synthesized which increased the yield in terms of incorporation of DNA. He was thinking primarily about the virology meetings.

He had moved from Carolyn's apartment back out to his house across the bridge on West Island in the lake. The night of September 10 he went to bed early. When the alarm went off at four, Paul realized he was going to have a headache. He took two 500 milligram tablets of acetaminophen with his vitamins and had an extra cup of coffee. After he had shaved and packed his suitcase, Paul checked his briefcase to make sure he had his manuscript and slides. Then he put his THC and a hairbrush in the briefcase along with two books to read on the flight and snapped it shut.

He took the limousine to the airport. The flight was from Cleveland to New York, then, after changing planes, to Madrid and Rome. He checked his suitcase at the ticket counter and carried his raincoat and briefcase on board with him. He took a window seat in front of the wing, where it was quieter. After snapping on his harness belt in the rearward facing seat, he took out the copy of *Fast Reaction Techniques in Biochemistry* and started to read. In ten minutes they were airborne. Paul still had a headache, and the more he tried to read the worse it felt. So he put the book in his briefcase and looked out the window. He felt nervous about the trip.

The little boy sitting beside him was arguing with his parents. They handed the child a copy of *Life* which he opened and stared at for a minute. Then he dropped it on the floor and started whining again. Paul picked the magazine up and leafed through it, appreciating the large pictures and brief text. Then he put it down. He closed his eyes.

At Kennedy Airport Paul knew he was not going to be able to do any useful reading on the flight to Madrid, so he checked his briefcase. His suitcase was already ticketed straight through to Rome. He slept on and off during most of the flight to Madrid and did not deplane during the stopover. He was annoyed at the length of the trip and wished they hadn't banned the supersonic transports.

It was dark in Rome when they landed at Fiumicino Airport, although it was only afternoon in Cleveland. Paul waited at the carousel for his baggage. He spotted the suitcase and picked it up. When the baggage stopped arriving and his briefcase did not appear, he asked a porter to trace it. The porter made a phone call, smiled, and assured Paul that they would have it located in about five minutes. An hour later it had not turned up. Paul checked his bag through customs, went to the airport manager's office, stepped in, and complained to the woman in the outer office. She punched the code data from Paul's ticket and baggage stub into the desk console. The screen lit up, showing that the bag had definitely been put aboard at Kennedy. She said it's got to be here somewhere, unless they offloaded it at Madrid. He thanked her for pointing out the obvious. She asked him if he was in a hurry. He said no, since it was still before dinner, body time, and the twenty-minute train to Naples ran round the clock. She told him to check back in an hour. He went out and changed his dollars for lire.

An hour and twenty minutes later she still hadn't found the briefcase. Paul explained that his papers and slides were in it, and that was the reason he always carried it personally on a flight instead of checking it. She gave him a funny look, and said they would pay for a hotel room in Rome if he wished. She offered to call him the minute the briefcase turned up. Just as well to wait here, he thought. If I tell them to forward it to Naples, they'll only lose it again.

Paul checked into a hotel and switched on the TV in his room, but he couldn't understand a thing. He turned from channel to channel, but they were all in Italian. There was even an American film dubbed in Italian. Suddenly he got a sinking feeling. His THC was in the briefcase. He jumped up and reached for the phone, but realized there was nothing to do but wait. He went down to the coffee shop in the hotel and had a light meal. By this time it was the middle of the night, Rome time. Paul began to feel panicky. I can't call up a physician at this time of night, he thought, but I could walk into the emergency room of a hospital. He convinced himself that he was behaving childishly. Besides, Jordan had said that the half-life of the THC-12 in the human body was thirty-eight hours. So he still had most of it in his bloodstream. He went up to his room and went to sleep.

·11·

MARCO

IN THE MORNING he got up, showered and dressed, but didn't shave. He went downstairs for breakfast. He noticed vaguely that he could understand the conversations that floated through the room, and for a moment that seemed odd.

He packed up and checked out. He looked down at the receipt the desk clerk gave him and said in Italian that it was the wrong name, that his name was not Marco Capelli. The day clerk apologized and took the receipt back. He asked for the room number. The key said 36. The clerk showed him the ledger. Beside "36" the flowing script said "Marco Capelli." The clerk asked him what the correct name was. *"Mi scusi,"* he said, and walked out holding the receipt.

He took a taxi to the station and caught the train to Milan. After a short subway ride, he was walking through the streets around the university. He went to his apartment and tried his keys. They didn't fit. Frowning, he walked with his suitcase a few blocks and knocked on Alexa's door. He heard footsteps and the door opened.

When she saw him she looked startled, then threw her arms around his neck and kissed him over and over again, tears streaming down her face. She led him into the kitchen where she was eating breakfast. Marco was overwhelmed at seeing her. He had thought he would never see her again. She forgot her breakfast. They went into the little bedroom and Alexa drew the curtains. She took off her dress and hugged and kissed Marco. He took his clothes off and they got into bed and made love.

Afterward, they lay and listened to the sounds of voices and bicycles and cars. The sunlight was pushing at the curtains, but the room was dusky. She asked where he had been for months, and he said he couldn't say. They got dressed and went out, hand in hand, like children. They passed the open air market and stopped to buy fruits and vegetables. When evening came, they were still talking. I'm home, thought Marco.

"Where have you been? Your course starts in a few days. A man your age behaving this way. No wonder you foul up. You're irresponsible and a daydreamer. I'm glad you shaved your beard off." Tullio Bellini looked carefully at the stubble on Marco's chin. "Anyway, welcome back. I can't imagine why you didn't tell anyone." Tullio gave Marco a hug. They loved each other almost as father and son. "Can you come for dinner tonight? Or we can eat out."

"No," said Marco. "I'm going to be with Alexa. She's singing at Trattoria Degli Angeli. Tomorrow perhaps."

They walked around the cloistered courtyard enclosed by the low buildings of the Physics Department and stopped at the marble fountain in the center.

"Marco, I hardly know how to tell you this, but I thought you were dead." Tullio put his hands on Marco's shoulders, but he couldn't look at his face. "I don't know why I thought that. I'm getting old, and I think of death too often."

Marco wondered if Tullio knew what it was to *really* be obsessed with thoughts of death. They walked into the department office. Tullio told the secretary to issue Marco new keys to his office and the building, and to the fusion reactor complex. Then he just stood there and looked at Marco. His eyes were red, and he put on his sunglasses. They stood there facing each other until the secretary came back with the keys.

Marco sat in the wire-backed chair sipping Pernod, a habit he had picked up while doing postdoctoral work at the Sorbonne. Around the small table were Carlo, Luisa, and Simone, three of his dear friends, exchanging reminiscences about their August holidays. Alexa came out on the stage with her guitar and sat on the stool. Slender and graceful with small breasts, the sight of her always excited Marco. She had long, straight black hair and a small mouth, and wore contact lenses over her brown eyes when she performed, although she could barely see the audience through the bright haze created by the spotlights. She adjusted the microphones, tapped them to make sure they were live, and pressed a switch with her toe so that she was bathed in red light. She looks incredibly beautiful, thought Marco.

Alexa sang songs in Italian, and old English and Irish ballads. They seemed to have a deeper meaning for Marco than they ever had before. He watched her fingers on the guitar frets. They were delicate, but she played with feeling and precision.

Then she smiled at Marco and announced a special treat to the audience. Her lover would play for them. Marco panicked. Could he play? It had been months. But he hopped up on the stage and took the guitar, removed the capo, and bowed as though at a formal concert. Alexa sat on the stool while Marco stood with the guitar. They sang one of the songs from Marco's student days. The fingernails on his right hand were too short, but the music filled the room. It was a sad tune that ended unresolved in the dominant seventh. Marco leaned over and kissed her on the mouth. There was applause from the small audience.

Alexa looked very sad indeed. "I know you don't have to tell me, and I won't ask again, but I don't understand why you refuse to tell me where you were. Only, don't tell me if you were with another woman."

"I was in Sorrento. I was alone, and I read a lot." That seemed reasonable to Marco, although he was not very sure it was true. It seemed to be true, but it was hard to remember.

"You can come and go as you please, but it's such a puzzle that you gave me the money to rent the cabin and then disappeared."

"The cabin?"

"In the woods, in Maremma. You know, the one Luisa told us about."

He did remember. It was odd that he had forgotten. "That was thoughtless. I'm sorry."

"Marco?"

"What?"

"I rented it through September."

"My class starts in a few days."

"But you've taught the course before. How much preparation do you need?"

"I should look it over."

"Why don't you bring some books, and we can drive to the cabin for two days. It would be a shame if the money were all wasted."

"Yes, it would be a shame." Marco was touching Alexa's dark hair. He wondered how he could have left her behind just to go to Sorrento. "We should go. Let's go right now."

"Should we pack anything?"

"Is there food?"

"There are cans and a stove in the cabin. I drove up a few weeks ago."

"Let's just go."

He grabbed a few clothes he had left around Alexa's apartment, and she put some of hers into a sack. They ran to Marco's car, and with Alexa directing him they got there in four hours. The cabin was made of cement and white stones. It was on a dirt road back in the woods, and there was a pond two hundred meters away. Outside was a tank of compressed gas for the stove. There was no electricity.

They got out of the car, and there was no one around at all as far as they could tell. They smelled all the damp earth and tree smells of the woods, and they could hear birds. It was late in the afternoon.

Inside the cabin were two cots, a table and a bench, one old blanket and no sheets. The canned food was hardly more than survival rations, but there was running water pumped from a spring in back.

"Alexa. Alessandra," said Marco. He took her tunic off. Then he pulled his shirt over his head and stepped out of his pants. Alexa began to embrace him, but Marco walked out the door.

"Marco! Where are you going?"

"For a walk. Are you coming?"

"But you have no clothes on."

"I didn't think you noticed. Are you coming?" He was already walking past the car and down the dirt road. Alexa ran to catch up with him. She touched his back, but he didn't stop, so she ran up beside him and walked along.

"Marco, where are we going?"

"For a walk in the woods."

"I know, but suppose we meet someone, and we have no clothes on?"

"We say hello, and tell them that we are their new

neighbors, and invite them over to dinner to share our canned meat and vegetables."

"There is no meat."

"Then they can bring the meat. They should bring the meat, and the wine, since we have the bread."

"There is no bread."

He stopped and looked at her. "No bread? I thought you had the bread." They started to walk again, but she bumped him hard with her hip, and he almost stumbled off the road. They both began to laugh. Then they held hands, and Alexa began to hum a tune. In a minute she saw the pond ahead.

"The water may be cold."

"If it is, we'll feel warm when we get out." Marco picked her up in his arms and kept walking. Alexa put her arms around his neck and her face on his shoulder.

"You look like another man without your beard. Why did you shave it off?"

"So that you could have a new lover. Everyone needs a new lover sometime." Marco had walked into the water up to his waist. Then he dropped Alexa in. She yelled and splashed around, and looked mad. She dived under the water and pulled his legs so that he slipped under the water too.

They swam until they were out of breath, twice around the little pond that was deeper than their heads only in the middle. When they got out of the water the air felt warmer than before, but by the time they got back to the cabin they were chilled. There were several half-burned logs in the fireplace which Marco started easily, and they sat in front of the fire with the blanket over their shoulders.

Alexa put on her tunic and asked Marco to light the stove. Then she opened a couple of cans and mixed everything together in the pan. When it was ready, Marco looked at it.

"What is it?"

"Garbage."

He pretended to be repelled, but it smelled good and he was hungry. "We should eat garbage more often."

"It's not only good, it's inexpensive. The recipe comes to me from my grandmother."

When they had finished, Marco noticed that it was dark, although it was still early. He looked out the window and saw the storm clouds. "Alessandra, does the roof leak?"

"Perhaps. Why?"

"Because it's going to rain. And I have to close up the car." Marco ran out, but before he got back it was pouring. The roof didn't leak, but the rain falling on it made a lot of noise. After a while, though, it got to be soothing. Marco put two more logs on the fire, and they looked at one of the beds. It had an old horse hair mattress with holes and stains. When they turned it, the other side looked the same. So they lay down and covered themselves with the blanket. The fire warmed their heads, and its flickering light made Alexa seem to dance as she sat up. Then she pulled the blanket over her head and began to caress Marco with her mouth. They rolled on their sides and he did the same with his tongue, until

he found the special taste. She began to lubricate profuse-
ly. He turned and entered her. She had closed her eyes
and was biting her lip. He put his arms around her as far
as they would go, and she curled her legs around his. The
oral stimulation had gotten him so aroused that he came
very quickly.

"Alexa?" She was humming a song he didn't know.
"Alexa, did you come?"

"Oh, maybe."

"Tell me."

"Yes."

They were quiet for a long time and listened to the
rain. Then he said, "Shall I sleep on the other bunk?
This one is so small."

"But we have only one blanket."

"Oh. Well, perhaps you would like to sleep on the
other bunk then."

At this they began wrestling, and Marco slipped inside
of her again. It was so easy. She was always ready for
him and enjoyed making love as much as he did. They
would compliment one another, and wonder whether it
was possible that other couples enjoyed it as much. They
decided that they were probably exceptional in their sen-
suality and lucky to have found each other. Whenever
Marco moved, Alexa moved with such harmony that they
seemed to be directed by one will. Whatever one found
pleasurable, so did the other. Neither had had such an
experience with previous lovers. There had always been
with others some lack of communication, or a little sa-
dism, some disjunction of desire, and generally, after the

first, a loss of that childlike playfulness that made it fun.

They moved in one manner for a while, and then shifted position and went on. At times they were gentle, at times rough. The feeling was mutual. Periodically they would look at each other and smile, pull together, and kiss deeply. Marco brushed his lips over the fine down on her cheek and over her lips. The tips of their tongues touched briefly. Alexa laughed and hugged him so hard she forced his breath out, and he laughed also.

"Alexa, I love you."

"I love you too, Marco."

They were moving slowly. Suddenly Alexa began to pull downward each time Marco moved out, and in a short time he could feel he was on the verge of an orgasm.

"I'm going to come."

"I'm coming too, love."

His movements became harder and less voluntary. He could feel the pressure building up, and with one last thrust it broke loose. Alexa gasped and pressed his buttocks down on her. She was coming at the same time. The shocks ran through Marco, and he shuddered in a long series of convulsions.

Finally they lay still, drenched in perspiration. He bit her ear gently and let his head drop onto the mattress. They had made love for nearly an hour and were exhausted. It was chilly, so Alexa pulled the blanket up to cover them. They lay in each other's arms and went to sleep.

Later there was a blinding flash of light and a terrible

sound of thunder simultaneously. Marco sat up, his heart pounding. The light was still there.

"What happened," asked Alexa.

"Just thunder."

"But what's that light?"

Marco got up and went to the window. A tall tree near the road was burning, set afire from the lightning. Perhaps it will start the woods on fire, he thought. But the rain was coming down in torrents. Still, the tree blazed on and on, and Alexa came over and threw the blanket over them. Finally the fire began to grow smaller and Marco thought they would be safe. They crawled back into the small bed, in exactly the same position as before.

Marco could smell the dinner, the sweat, Alexa's hair, the smells of love, and the odor of the smoldering logs in the fireplace. He closed his eyes and was asleep.

Marco was to teach the course in classical mechanics for the second year in a row. He walked into the small lecture hall and looked at the students. He felt a strong bond for them immediately. He had never been happier than when he had sat where they were now.

"You are free to attend lecture or not, as you will. Our text is Shumsky's *Mechanics*. You can read it, or work on the teaching machines. I want you in this room only if you find my lectures helpful." He noted that every seat was taken. In spite of, or perhaps because of, his reputation, he was the most popular teacher in the department.

"You have previously seen mechanics developed from Newton's three laws, of which the first is actually due to

Galileo. To restate them: One. Every body remains at rest, or continues in a state of uniform motion in a straight line, unless acted on by an external force. Two. The time rate of change of momentum of a body is proportional to the vector sum of the external forces on it. Three. For every action, there is an equal reaction in the opposite direction.

"However, the most elegant approach to mechanics is to use the variational method developed in the eighteenth and nineteenth centuries by Lagrange and Hamilton." Marco wrote down the action integral and explained the significance of the Lagrangian. He derived the Euler-Lagrange equations.

"Now if we are concerned with a free particle, the Lagrangian is $p^2/2m$. You see, there is no potential energy term. More generally, you see that the first term in Lagrange's equations is the time rate of change of momentum," Marco was substituting one symbol for another, "and the second term is none other than the force on the particle, since the kinetic energy does not depend on position coordinates. Thus, in Cartesian coordinates, we recover Newton's second law, and the first law as well when the external force is zero."

The class was over. One of the students raised her hand and asked why classical mechanics was still required. "For two reasons," Marco answered. The students sat down again. "First, because it is easier to understand the Hamiltonian and the commutator in quantum mechanics if you first see the Hamiltonian and Poisson brackets in classical mechanics. And," he grinned broadly, "because the science was founded by Galileo, for whom I have a high personal regard."

In the following weeks, Marco took them through conservation of energy, momentum and angular momentum, and he explained reduced mass and the Kepler problem. He discussed collisions and linear and nonlinear oscillations. By this time three new students had to stand at the back of the class. He had stools brought in for them.

By now his beard had begun to grow out, and he looked just like his progenitor, Enzo Cigala. In Cigala's day, beards were fashionable among intellectuals and scientists. Today, Marco was one of the few members of Cigala's clone to wear one.

Thursdays Augusto Ottaviano came over from the Fermi Institute for a run on the fusion reactor, unless the machine was down. He was the best authority on plasmas and magnetohydrodynamics. The team comprised a dozen physicists, engineers, and graduate students. Although fast-pulsed fusion reactors had been in use for twenty years, the potentially more efficient continuous reactors had not yet been made to work.

Marco looked at the banks of dials and meters, and the modestly sized toroidal machine in the center of the large shed. Taped up on the wall was an old newspaper clipping and photographs of what was left after the fission breeder reactor overheated and blew in São Paulo, spreading radioactive vapor over the city. After that, all the other fission reactors had been shut down, except those over the continental shelves. It had taken this to shake loose enough funds to support an adequate fusion program.

The run was so-so. They achieved high enough temperatures and plasma densities, but the plasma confinement time was still an order of magnitude short of sustained fusion. At eight o'clock Marco, Tullio, Augusto, and three others went out to a small restaurant for dinner. They had bitter vermouth and antipasto, risotto and veal. After the fruit, they strolled down the way to get espresso and pastries. The topic had turned to the possibility of designing direct energy converters to replace the heat engine devices used by present reactors, which would result in a reduction in thermal pollution. As the evening wore on, Marco was less and less attentive to the technical discussion. He could hear his brothers calling one another.

It was happening again. Locked into mental register, the Clone Twos set scattered fires around the city. They were armed with the shotguns captured from the police during the previous skirmish. Marco, with his beard, looked at his two clean-shaven companions and felt a nagging near recollection.

When the firemen came, the Clone Twos opened up on them. Set on kill, the shotguns were lethal at fifty meters. The unarmed android firemen were shredded where they stood. Some took cover in their trucks, others ran. Several climbed into sewers and storm drains. Marco ran down the street with the two others, seeing what they saw, feeling their arms and legs swinging as they ran. The twenty-eight Clone Twos were a colony of interlaced minds, more clever than any one alone. But they were also warped. It was as though all the demons lurking in

*the unconscious had risen to the surface. There was a
heightened sense of awareness, but at the same time a
dropping away of individuality. In the background they
could feel the minds of the two children who were not
strongly enough coupled to commit themselves to the
pack.*

*They knew immediately when the police began to
move. Twenty-eight pairs of eyes made a network that
was hard to surprise. They began to disperse. Each went
his own way in the darkness, the greater mind dissolving
by degrees into many smaller minds.*

Marco was asleep in his apartment when he was awakened by a knock. There were two android policemen
facing him when he opened the door.

"Marco Capelli?"

"Yes."

"Will you please come with us? There is no hurry, but
please get dressed." He heard the rasp of voices over the
radio in their patrol van.

Marco was terrified. He wondered how many of the
others had been rounded up, and how they had known.
He tried to appear impassive, the respectable citizen
roused out of his bed in the middle of the night. At the
police station they took him into a room and put a wallet
and some keys on the table in front of him.

"Do you recognize these?" asked the human detective.
Marco opened the wallet. It smelled very bad. Inside
were his water-soaked driver's license, University I.D.
card, his credit cards, and pictures of his parents. He felt
his pockets. His wallet was still there. So were his keys.

"Are these yours?"

"Yes. Where did you get them?"

"There was a riot tonight."

"Yes, I heard."

"Almost seventy firemen were destroyed. One of the survivors found a decomposed body in a storm drain and the body had your wallet and these keys on it."

"I reported my things stolen over a month ago. You have the records. You must have found the man who stole them. Who was he?"

"The body was decomposed."

Marco looked around. They didn't seem suspicious. They probably just wanted to identify the body.

"How did he die?"

"Strangulation, it would appear. His neck was broken, and there was a wire wrapped around it. Did you know that the university reported you missing when you didn't pick up your pay check for two months?"

"I was away on vacation."

"Without telling anyone? Where?"

"Sorrento."

"Do you mind if we check your fingerprints?"

"No."

They took his fingerprints and fed them into the pattern analyzer. Marco's throat and mouth were very dry.

"Please fill out this receipt for the return of your stolen property." Marco filled it out and signed his name. The detective left the room saying, "There will be a short delay, a formality."

Twenty minutes later, the detective and a sleepy man in a blue suit came into the room where Marco was waiting. The detective spoke. "We searched your apartment and found this." He handed Marco an American passport. In it was a picture of a man without a beard and underneath was the name, "Paul Kyteler."

The man in the blue suit was speaking for a moment before Marco realized it was English.

"Dr. Kyteler, I said we've been looking for you since the middle of September. Your colleagues in Naples notified the American Embassy when you didn't arrive." It seemed that the whole scene was transpiring at some great distance and in slow motion. He watched the consular official's mouth open and close. The two men left the room. Then the American returned.

"Dr. Kyteler, the police have verified your identity through your fingerprints. That decomposed body was just a skeleton, but the police know it was Capelli because of the dental records. The police surgeon says it must have been in the storm drain long before you left Cleveland. They don't know why you were impersonating him, and they thought perhaps I did. They assume it's some kind of game involving the members of something they call a clone or clan." He took Paul's arm and led him out into the front room. The green letters glowed on the screen of the desk console: "DENTAL I D / MARCO CAPELLI / 40 / PHYSICIST / UNIV MILAN / NO ARRESTS // FINGERPRINT I D / CLONE 2 / PAUL KYTELER / 42 / BIOLOGIST / U S A / NO ARRESTS // CROSS CHECK MARCO CAPELLI PAUL KYTELER / BOTH CLONE 2 / 38 MEMBERS / 30 IN MILAN"

"In any event, since they are satisfied that you didn't

kill Capelli, we insisted that they release you. However, it would be helpful if you could provide us all with an explanation."

But Paul never did.

·12·

A MATTER OF MINDS

PAUL READ EVERYTHING on Enzo Cigala that he could find. Nobel laureate in physics, teacher and grand master of a whole generation of first rank physicists at the Fermi Institute in Milan. Especially interesting was the scholarly biography Paul had picked up at the Rome airport on the way back to Cleveland. He could now read it in Italian with the ease of a native.

Cigala had always been interested in biology, and fancied himself in the tradition of Schrödinger, Von Neuman, and Wiener. He had also been pathologically afraid of death and obsessed with the quest for immortality. He was driven by the widely held but vain hope that one lives on in one's works in some literal sense.

He saw the implications of cloning one day when visiting a friend who was developing a cloned strain of rhesus monkeys. He found that others had been pursuing the idea for several years, and used his influence to get an appointment to the Human Cloning Planning Project. After the first successful live birth, which established Clone One, Cigala persuaded his mistress to submit to a nuclear transplant with himself as the donor. He stood by while the baby was born, and used to stare down into the boy's eyes. Having read the histories of identical twins recounted in 1883 by Sir Francis Galton in his *Inquiries into Human Faculty and Its Development,* Cigala was sure there would be mental contact and that his soul would be transmitted into the future by his son, the closest son a man could have. But telepathic union never developed, and at eight years of age the boy accidentally drowned. Cigala became withdrawn after that, and abandoned his work on symmetry principles to turn his attention to robots. He extended Boolean algebra and developed the algebraic theory of forms that unified symbolic linguistics and automata theory. It was his work, more than that of any other, which set the stage for the development of modern androids. He believed that consciousness was an inseparable concomitant of any information handling system that could learn, perceive and reason. About emotion he was not so sure, but having undergone a life of inner torment, he seemed to regard that as a potential blessing. Cigala died without ever achieving his own literal immortality, although his cells live on in tissue culture. He was buried next to his father, the distinguished conductor of the Vienna State Opera Orchestra.

Paul had been tapering off on the THC without telling Jordan. He kept trying to open the door in his mind, to establish waking telepathic contact with the other Clone Twos, but with no success. One morning at eight-thirty he suddenly began to talk to someone. This person seemed to be asleep and dreaming.

In the dream Paul asked him who he was.

"Ben Rose."

"Where do you live?"

"Right here in San Diego."

"I'm a biologist. Would you like to visit my lab sometime?"

"Yes."

"What do you do?"

"Aerospace engineering."

Paul had been incorporated as a character in the dream, and as it moved on, he was dismissed. He tried, but the contact was gone.

It was easy to locate Benjamin Rose. When Paul phoned him and recited the dream fragment, he was astonished. Paul asked him if he was a Clone Two and the answer was affirmative. He became excited about the prospect of investigating telepathy and flew in to stay with Paul in his house on the artificial island in Lake Erie. He looked exactly the way Paul had a decade earlier. They then began an increasingly successful series of experiments on voluntary telephathic transmission.

While Paul had been gone, Carolyn had filed suit on behalf of Terry and Desmond in federal district court, naming the county clerk as defendant for failure to issue a marriage license. She planned to base her suit on the Fourteenth Amendment equal protection clause; on the

Civil Rights Act of 1886, which prohibits any person, under color of any statute of any state, from depriving a person within U.S. jurisdiction of his rights under the Constitution; and on *Loving* v. *Virginia,* the 1967 decision which had the effect of striking down laws prohibiting miscegenation. She was requesting a writ of *mandamus* to require the county clerk to issue the marriage license.

Now that the case was coming to trial, Carolyn was openly working from her downtown office. Her two partners, to their credit, had backed her completely and were helping her to prepare. Business or no, they realized that the decision would be an historic one, and that the case could well reach the Supreme Court on appeal. Angelo had lined up several expert witnesses to testify on their behalf, including a prominent psychiatrist with considerable trial experience.

It was Tuesday, and Carolyn had asked Paul to come over from Eagle Memorial to her office for lunch. The clerk had just brought in sandwiches and coffee. They were sitting on maroon vinyl-covered chairs in the book-lined room with a thick shag rug on the floor. Angelo popped in to check a citation and left again.

"While you were amusing yourself in Italy, we've been keeping very busy." Carolyn grinned. "You know, we have a formidable opponent. Since my plaintiffs are suing a state official, the defense is being handled by the state attorney general's office. Litchfield is a man of no small political ambitions, and I may be turning him into our next governor."

She kicked her shoes off and ran her toes through the nap of the carpeting. "It's almost pathetic in a way. The county clerk is a sweet little lady of ninety-one with the unlikely name of Emily Hugely. She's caught in the middle. When I spoke to her, she said she wished she had retired last year so she could have avoided all of this publicity."

"Are you going to win?"

"I don't know, but we're very lucky to have gotten Judge Jackson."

"Why?"

"If I read her correctly, she may allow us to present our whole case. She has a liberal record. Many judges would throw us out without a hearing." Then she became very serious. "Paul, will you please keep this telepathy business quiet?"

"Why should I?"

"Because it could be used against us in court."

"I don't see how."

"Don't you understand you've discovered one thing that people can do that androids can't? All they have to do is argue that humans have extrasensory perception and androids don't. The identification of an undeniably mental difference between humans and androids could turn the case against us."

"But most people are not telepathic, and may never be."

"Yes, but whether it's true or not, they would argue that it's within the reach of all humans to do it."

"I'm not the only potential source. Sooner or later the

story will get out."

"It could be later."

She turned and stared out the tinted window of the eighty-third-story office, watching the shuttle copters sparkle against the clear sky as they took off and landed on the rooftops.

Paul got up and stretched. The early afternoon sun was making him drowsy. "When does your case come to trial?"

"A week from tomorrow."

"And what makes you think androids do not have ESP?"

She looked up at him in surprise. "Do they?"

Anna had just left the lab after watching her embryo for ten minutes. It was now at the four-cell stage and would be ready very soon. They were using an image intensifier so that they could use low light levels in the phase contrast microscope. They didn't want to cook it.

Paul sat down at his desk, where he had *Elementary Principles of Android Design* opened to the middle of chapter three. He phoned upstairs to Tung. "James, what do you know about androids?"

"Lots. My mother was one. Seriously, though, I did my thesis on brain circuitry in androids. That's how I first got interested in people."

"Will you be there for a while? I'm coming up."

When Paul walked in, Jordan was sitting cross-legged on his desk in his sneakers and jeans. "Going under my head, huh? What's up? And how the hell are you?"

"Fine. Oh, and I meant to tell you. THC is for the weak in spirit and the faint of heart. I found something better."

"What? Getting laid every hour?"

"No. The mind is a door to a vast new world."

Tung walked in from the other lab. His bloody hands indicated he had been helping Lucille implant her electrodes. He wiped them on his lab coat. "I heard that. You have now entered the innermost circle."

"Not really. Read this." Paul handed them copies of the letter he had written to *Nature* asserting the existence of ESP in humans. It refrained from mentioned the riots, but detailed his recent experiments with Benjamin Rose, emphasizing the fact that they were members of the same human clone. After they had read the manuscript, he related the actual events that had transpired in Milan, as well as his "dream" about the first riot.

"Oh, Christ!" said Jordan. "That means that every psychological experiment ever done is in question."

"Probably not. It seems to me that this has emerged as a significant factor only with the development of clones. Before that, who knows. It was likely a weak influence at best. Certainly none of the previous studies on ESP can compare with what I've been able to do with Dr. Rose."

"But why would your clone want to destroy androids if Enzo Cigala was their creator?"

"My whole clone shares Cigala's abnormal preoccupation with death. Both Clone Twos and androids are in a sense Cigala's children, and there is a natural sibling rivalry. The Clone Twos couldn't stand the idea that androids were immortal while they were not. I felt this, too, even though, unlike most Clone Twos, I didn't know about my connection with Cigala. During telepathic union, the aggregate personality seems to amplify unconscious hatreds and jealousies. In the case of the Clone Twos in Milan, there were so many of them in one location, the interaction was so intense, that they were led to act out their unconscious hostilities toward androids. It's hard to explain to someone who has never experienced it what it's like to lose one's own identity in a mass of fused minds, to become part of a larger, and malignant, organism.

"Until recently, superficially I believed that androids were machines without genuine minds, but underneath, I knew that they were real people. I couldn't bear the thought that they would all be alive after I died. In order to hate them, I had to depersonalize them and consider them less than human. It was particularly easy to do, since society at large subscribes to that idea anyway. But now I feel so damn guilty about what my clone has done to them, I intend to do something to help make up for it."

"I suppose that explains the other 'mass hysteria' riots and the Japanese suicides," replied Jordan. "Each clone must have its own particular quirk, something that really bugs it, the kind of thing each of us can usually keep under control as an isolated individual, unless he's a psychopath. Since the members of a clone are all of the same sex, I can understand why only women were involved in Geneva. But Paul, these clones are positively dangerous, especially yours, My god, man, what are we going to do with you?"

"Distance seems to weaken the effect. That's why the disturbances were localized, I think. Besides, we can probably learn to control it. And there are other clones who haven't got themselves into trouble yet, and may never do so."

Paul had been staring out of the window as he talked. He turned and tossed a copy of Carolyn's trial notes on the desk. Jordan leafed through it, then Tung. "Look, Michael, about this civil rights case, I think James can help."

"So now you want to steal my postdoc."

Paul turned to Tung. "Can androids communicate tele-pathically?"

"I don't think so. I'll ask one."

"I want you to design and build a rig so that a couple of androids can communicate with each other. Just a simple FM radio transmitter and receiver to be implanted in their brains. I want it to be as private to them as possible."

"That I can do. I'll use matched crystals to produce the carrier frequency. Since their brain temperature remains constant, the frequency will be stable. I can even make it short range and directional."

"No, don't do that. Will they be able to speak to each other without giving any external sign?"

"Yep."

"How long will it take?"

"A couple of weeks."

"Too long. How about six days?"

Tung looked at Jordan. "With some friends helping, maybe six days."

"Can you implant the units here if I bring the subjects in?"

"Yep."

"I'll have them here Tuesday evening."

As he walked out the door, Paul could hear Jordan muttering, "Oh well, this month has been a total loss already. We never have anything important to do around here anyway."

·13·

THE TRIAL

THURSDAY MORNING PAUL BLEW the secret. He released a written text about human telepathy to the reporters and then agreed to a TV press conference. The news media treated the story with the kind of skepticism that had attended Linus Pauling's claim that vitamin C could influence colds. He had already written to Alexa and Tullio giving them partial explanations. After all, he was all that was left of Marco.

Friday afternoon Paul got a call from the state attorney general's office, requesting a meeting, immediately if possible, in town. He agreed. Litchfield insisted that they meet in the vault of the Mercantile Bank, which seemed a peculiar place, but since the attorney general had taken the bait, Paul had no complaint.

Litchfield had the vault door closed behind them. "I wanted absolute secrecy and security, so I chose the bank."

"I see. Can you tell me what you want? I'm not used to playing spy games."

"You realize your wife and I are on opposite sides in this so-called civil rights case."

"Ex-wife."

"You see her frequently, and we regard that as an indication of a continuing liaison."

"You can draw any conclusions you wish."

"What I want to know is whether you were serious yesterday morning or whether this is a hoax."

"I was serious."

"Can you prove it?"

"Right now there is a Clone Two named Benjamin Rose sitting at the desk in my house dictating into a recorder everything that is happening to me. Two newspaper reporters are with him. We plan to continue this for a week."

Litchfield opened up his briefcase and took out a card which said, "Do not speak." Pasted underneath was a reproduction of one of the surrealistic paintings of the fifteenth-century Dutchman, Hieronymus Bosch. Litchfield put it away. "Am I making myself clear?"

"Yes."

"Now if this turns out, I will want you to testify for the state. Will you testify against your wife's clients?"

"Why not? I've always disliked androids. Anyone can tell you that."

"I could call you as a hostile witness. Or I could subpoena the recording at your house and compare it with this one." He pulled a small audio recorder out of his pocket.

"I've told you I'll testify. Do you want anything else?"

"No. My office has your house bugged, and if what you say about yourself and this other Clone Two is true, we already have the evidence. Just be in court at the Federal Building Wednesday morning." He pressed the alarm button next to the giant steel door, and the bank president let them out of the vault. Paul shook Litchfield's hand. Litchfield must have thought Paul was smiling at him, but Paul was smiling at himself.

Court convened at ten o'clock Wednesday. At the plaintiffs' table were Desmond, Terry, Carolyn, and Angelo. With the court's permission, and over the objection of Litchfield, the national office of the American Civil Liberties Union had filed an *amicus curiae* brief which provided strong support for Carolyn's case. The ACLU argued the applicability of the Fourteenth Amendment equal protection clause to androids, and in addition contended that administrative procedures had deprived androids of their right to due process, also guaranteed under the Fourteenth Amendment.

The judge was a black woman named Chloe Jackson. She looked all business and no humor. Perhaps it was the importance of the case and her absolute intention to avoid reversible error. She sat down and rapped her gavel once. The courtroom was already quiet.

"This morning we will hear pretrial motions. Are plaintiffs and defendant ready?"

Litchfield rose from the table where he was sitting with two of his assistants and Miss Hugely. "Your honor,

I move to dismiss on the grounds that plaintiffs have failed to state a claim.''

"I will hear arguments on the motion.''

Carolyn stood up. "Your honor, such a motion is likely to rest on precisely the points of law at issue in the suit itself.''

"Court stands in temporary recess. Will attorneys for plaintiffs and defendant please join me in chambers?''

When they came back in, they remained standing. Judge Jackson gaveled once. "I rule against defendant's motion. However, the court recognizes defendant's right to renew it at any later time. Are there any further motions? If not, court stands adjourned until ten o'clock tomorrow morning. As this is a request for a writ of *mandamus*, you understand that there will be no jury.''

After Litchfield and his associates had left the room, Paul and Ben, as well as several others including Martin, the red-haired android, came up to the table where Carolyn was collecting her things. "What happened?'' asked Paul.

Carolyn started putting papers in her briefcase. "The judge wanted an off the record discussion of the motion and others that Litchfield was prepared to make. So we had a little informal chat in the library. Litchfield insisted that the entire action be dismissed as having no legal basis. But Judge Jackson agreed with me that the motion hinged on the very issue to be raised during the trial. Then Litchfield tried to get Terry dismissed as a plaintiff on the grounds that an android is not a legal entity and has no standing in court. Judge Jackson said she would also not accept that motion, and for the same reason. Litchfield looked upset. I think he really thought the judge might dismiss. Finally he requested that in ruling on the motion, Judge Jackson make it clear for the record that he reserves the right to renew the objection later. She said she would, and of course, that it was his prerogative anyway. She said if he wanted to reintroduce the motion after presentation of evidence, she would hear it again and might rule on it then. She also reminded both of us that she had the privilege of dismissing either plaintiff at any time during the proceedings."

"What does it mean?" asked Desmond.

"It means we've won an important first step, the right to present our case. It doesn't guarantee anything about the final outcome."

When the trial began, Carolyn and Litchfield made their opening statements, in which they outlined the arguments they believed supported their respective positions. Then Carolyn began presenting witnesses. This occupied three days. It was just as well, since it was taking longer than expected to get the radio transmitters and receivers constructed. The psychiatrist that Angelo had located gave an especially moving account of the consciousness of robots, seasoned with clinical observations and anecdotes. Even under cross-examination he continued to strengthen Carolyn's case, so Litchfield quickly dismissed him.

Terry was on the stand for a whole day. Litchfield kept interrupting with objections, but Carolyn nonetheless was able to draw out testimony that would obviously have moved a jury, had there been one. Litchfield refused to cross-examine her at all, since to do so would have been to create the impression that he regarded her as a witness, and therefore as a person.

Carolyn called experts on the design, production, and training of androids who assured the court that they were in every important way as human as humans.

After the Sunday recess, Litchfield began his presentation, and countered Carolyn witness by witness. He, too, had a psychiatrist, and a clinical psychologist, as well as design engineers, who kept stressing the mechanical nature of robots and the way their personalities and responses were merely mechanistic functions of their components and circuitry.

This went on for the better part of two days, and then Litchfield called Paul to the stand. Ben Rose was seated in a room in another part of the building. A TV projector was set up, and Ben's image was thrown on a screen in the courtroom.

"Dr. Kyteler, you claim to be telepathic?"

"Yes, I am."

"Can you prove it?"

"Yes. Show me anything. Dr. Rose will draw or describe it. You can see the results immediately on the screen."

"First I want to make it clear for the record that attorney for the plaintiffs is your ex-wife."

"She is."

"And you are testifying even so, of your own accord?"

"Yes."

Paul was shown various drawings and pictures, quotations, even a blank sheet of paper. On the large TV projection, Ben immediately reproduced or recited each one. When the blank page came up, Ben laughed. The judge seemed impressed.

"Since there is a long history of illusion and stage magic, I have gathered a group of experts who are now in the courtroom and elsewhere in the building and who will testify that this display was in no way faked." Litchfield turned to look at Carolyn. "Unless plaintiffs will so stipulate at this point."

Carolyn went into a whispered conference at the table with Terry and Desmond. "We so stipulate," she said.

Litchfield turned to the judge. "That concludes our testimony, your honor."

Carolyn stood up. "Your honor, we have a rebuttal witness. It is obvious that defendant will later try to argue that humans are different from androids because only humans have extrasensory perception. We can prove otherwise."

Terry took the stand. Martin was seated at the back of the room with his face to the wall. Carolyn took Litchfield's set of pictures and showed them one by one to Terry. Martin drew each one exactly, and in the correct order. His drawings were brought up for the judge to compare with the originals, and entered as exhibits. Carolyn sat down.

"If the court please," began Litchfield, "the two tests were not exactly comparable." Beads of sweat stood out on his face in the cool courtroom. He wiped his brow

with a handkerchief. "Mr. Rose is located in a room two
floors up and at the other end of the building. I suggest
that the demonstration be repeated with the second android sitting in front of the TV camera so that we all can
see."

In a few minutes, Martin appeared in the TV projection with his bright red hair and sat down. "Your honor,
it will suit me if the same pictures are used as long as
their order is shuffled again," said Litchfield.

Carolyn showed the first picture to Terry. Martin sat
immobile, waiting. She tried another. Nothing happened.
There was absolutely no communication. After a while,
the judge terminated the proceedings for the day, and
Carolyn knew she had lost.

She, Paul, Desmond, and Terry took the elevator two
flights up. Paul was thinking, Tung assured me those
were not short-range transmitters. What could have happened? They walked down a corridor, past several reporters and various experts on the occult, and came to the
room at the end of the hall. Two policemen were guard-
ing the door. They opened it for the delegation. When he
stepped in, Paul saw a smaller room inside the first room.
The door to the little room was opened for them, and
they saw Martin and the TV camera facing each other.
Paul stepped back out of the little room and looked at its
outside walls. They were covered with a fine mesh copper
screen. They had Martin in a giant Faraday cage! Oh,
goddamn it all to hell! he thought. Of course the radio
signal couldn't get through. Now I know why Litchfield
had me meet him in that steel tomb in the bank: to make

sure *I* wasn't rigging it with a radio signal. I let a clever prick like Litchfield outsmart me, and he didn't even do it on purpose. He used the cage just to make sure his *own* demonstration was unimpeachable.

They were holding hands, dancing in a large circle in a clearing in the woods. "Why will play death?" asked one. "I will," said Sprague as he danced into the center of the circle with his drainage tube dangling from his nostril. He rushed this way and that, trying to touch the circle dancers. They could back away, but they had to keep holding hands. As Sprague touched them, one by one, they dropped to the ground.

Then Paul was in the center of the circle of dancers. There were all there, Laughton, Jean and Nadya, Martin, Terry and Desmond, Tung, Greg and Olivia, Guth, Litchfield, Anna and René, even Carolyn and Jordan, Alexa and Tullio. Then they peeled off their rubber masks. Underneath, all their faces were Paul's face. The circle danced round and round him, coming closer. He whirled around, and there was Marco with a sword in his hand. He swung the sword down and sliced Paul from the chest to the crotch. As Paul peered into the gaping slit, he could see wires and terminals, printed circuits and synthetic muscle, all framed by plastic connective tissue and skin.

Paul woke up and realized it had been just an ordinary nightmare, the kind everyone has. *"I know,"* thought Ben, who was sitting up in the darkness across the room. *"But it gives me an idea."* He flipped on the light, picked up the phone, and placed a call to San Diego. When he got an answer he said, "Give me *Ozma II.*"

When court reconvened, Carolyn asked for a one-day recess to bring in new witnesses from out of state. Her request was granted.

The following morning there were two intricate pieces of electronic gear in the courtroom. Each was a steel and plastic enclosure, rack mounted and on motor driven wheels. Each had two TV cameras and a display screen, and was connected via plastic tubing to circulating pumps and baths mounted at the bottoms of the racks. The two units, similar but not replicas, were also linked together by electrical cables.

Carolyn began. "Your honor, we have additional testimony to offer, directly pertinent to the points made the day before yesterday by both plaintiffs and defendant."

"Proceed."

"I would like to call Dr. Benjamin Rose as a witness for the plaintiffs." He took the stand. "Would you please state your name and occupation?"

"Benjamin Rose, life support systems design engineer, General Dynamics Corporation, San Diego."

"It was you we watched two days ago on the TV screen, was it not?"

"Yes, it was."

"Will you please tell the court something about the work you are engaged in?"

"I am working on the starship *Ozma II,* which we hope will fly for Tau Ceti within the next few years."

"How far away is Tau Ceti?"

"It's a star in the same class as our sun and is eleven light years away. With the acceleration the ion engines can produce, the round trip will take about eighty years, elapsed Earth time."

"Why do you call it *Ozma II?* Was there an *Ozma I?*"

"The name *Ozma* derives from the early days of radio astronomy when unsuccessful attempts were made to detect radio signals from other civilizations within our galaxy. We expect the Tau Ceti system to contain planets, and we hope to find at least primitive life forms.

"Will you tell us what we see at the side of the courtroom?" Carolyn gestured toward the electronic gear.

"That is part of the brain of *Ozma II.* It will control all shipboard functions and conduct the experiments and observations upon arrival."

"Is there anything unusual about it?"

"Most of the brain is composed of units like the one on the right, which is a large android brain designed so as to be mounted directly into racks in the starship. You can see that we did not bother to make the android look like a human. There will be twenty-four of these units in the starship control complex, and they will be augmented with 10^{13} bits of information storage capacity in crystal hologram and standing wave laser modules."

"And the object on the left is another such unit?"

"Not exactly. The starship brain is a hybrid. It is composed of a human brain interfaced with the twenty-four android brains, or if you will, with one large android brain consisting of twenty-four subunits. The left hand unit is the human brain, Dr. Lloyd Fahy."

The crowd in the courtroom was obviously shocked and began to whisper. Judge Jackson rapped her gavel.

"Now let me get this clear," said Carolyn. "You could not accomplish your objective with an android brain alone?"

"Oh yes, we could. Theoretically there is nothing cognitive a human can do that an android can't. But we are prohibited by federal law from training androids in the sciences. And scientific data in computer memory storage would not suffice. The starship mission must be controlled by a trained scientist. Of course, in order to construct a hybrid composed of a human interfaced with an android brain, we had to remove the rest of Dr. Fahy's body. This also allows us to avoid potential medical problems that might arise with a human body, even though the Lorentz transformation will make the travel time for the ship's occupants less than the eighty years elapsed Earth time. Let me say," Ben faced the judge, "that we tried to obtain a waiver of federal regulations. We even thought of constructing an all-android unit on one of the planetary colonies. But we found that international conventions are in accord with U.S. law concerning androids. In any event," Ben turned back to face Carolyn, "Dr. Fahy was willing, actually eager, to volunteer. The brain has been under construction for three years."

"And what is your job?" asked Carolyn.

"I am part of the life support team. In particular, I am in charge of designing gas, nutrient, and waste exchange systems for the brain."

"And what have you found recently?"

Ben looked at Paul, then folded his hands and looked at Litchfield.

"Why are you reluctant to tell us?"

"I am afraid it could jeopardize the mission and the entire space program."

"Then why did you volunteer to testify today?"

"Because after discussing it with Dr. Fahy, he insisted."

"What have you discovered recently?" Carolyn repeated.

"We found that the human part of the brain had taught everything it knows to the android part. Or, to be more exact, we found that there are no longer two interfaced brains, there is only one brain, part cellular and part synthetic. The localization of function that we began with has disappeared."

Carolyn walked back to her table and shuffled through some papers. She obviously wanted to let the effect of the words sink in. Then she walked back to the witness stand.

"Would you say you qualify as an expert on this brain?"

"There are only about four or five others who know as much about it as I do."

"Is there anything else we should know about the brain of *Ozma II?*"

"Yes. Since there is no localization of function, the destruction of any of the synthetic part would impair the cognitive functioning of the cellular part as it now exists.

There is something else as well. But I think you should ask Dr. Fahy himself."

Ben got down. Carolyn said, "I call Dr. Lloyd Fahy to the stand."

Litchfield jumped up. "I object, your honor. That machine is obviously not a suitable witness."

Carolyn replied, "Your honor, the Princeton definition established that it is the brain and the mind that constitute a person, not his appendages."

"Objection overruled," said Judge Chloe Jackson.

Ben went over and disconnected the wires that linked the two motorized equipment racks. The one on the left began to roll of its own accord toward the witness stand, stopped, turned to face the gallery, and backed up slightly.

"Will you please identify yourself for the court?" asked Carolyn.

The green letters appeared on the face of the display screen: "LLOYD FAHY, PH.D. IN GEOLOGY, PH.D. IN MICROBIOLOGY. RESIDENCE: GENERAL DYNAMICS CORPORATION, SAN DIEGO, CALIFORNIA."

"Do you confirm the testimony given by Dr. Rose?"

"YES. I AND MY 24 ANDROID COLLEAGUES WILL FLY THE STARSHIP OZMA TO TAU CETI, MAKE OBSERVATIONS, COLLECT SAMPLES, AND RETURN. WE WILL ALSO TRANSMIT OUR FINDINGS BY RADIO SO THAT EARTH WILL BEGIN TO RECEIVE INFORMATION ABOUT 51 YEARS AFTER WE START OUR VOYAGE."

"Do you have anything to add to what Dr. Rose has told us?"

"YES. MY ANDROID COLLEAGUE CAN READ MY MIND WHILE HE IS IN THE ELECTROMAGNETICALLY SHIELDED ROOM UPSTAIRS." There appeared on the display screen a large arrow pointing to the other rack-mounted unit. Again Judge Jackson had to gavel for order.

The other unit rolled out of the swinging doors at the back of the courtroom. In a few minutes it rolled into view on the TV projection screen near the witness stand. The demonstration involved showing the cards with the pictures and sentences to Fahy's TV cameras. In each case, an exact copy appeared immediately on the display screen mounted in the android unit visible in the TV projection.

Carolyn faced Judge Jackson. "Your honor, we, too, have various witnesses who will testify as to the authenticity of the demonstration we have just seen, and witnesses who will verify that the unit in the room upstairs in fact contains an android brain."

Litchfield looked tired and discouraged. He stipulated that it would not be necessary to call the witnesses. Then he again made the motion to dismiss on the grounds that plaintiffs had failed to state a claim. He obviously expected the motion to be denied. It was.

·14·

THE DECISION

ON THE LAST DAY of the trial, both plaintiffs and defendant made their closing statements.

Carolyn looked nervous and her voice was taut. "Your honor, I believe that we have established that androids are persons under the law in the way the law should be interpreted. What is it that distinguishes man from animal? The power of human cognition, not the size and shape of their bodies. We have heard expert testimony that, with regard to cognition, androids are the equal of biological humans. More than that, they express the full range of feelings and emotions that we have come to recognize in persons. They experience pain and fear, and if it were not for the emotion of love," she turned to face Terry and Desmond, "my android client would not be seeking the marriage license she desires.

"Attorney for the defendant had several witnesses describe at length how the mechanistic features of 'robots,' as he likes to call them, completely determine their personalities and behavior. This very dispute, involving the apparent discrepancy between mechanistic determinism on the one hand and free will on the other, has raged for centuries *with regard to human beings themselves.* Today we know that living creatures are, insofar as their behavior is concerned, nothing but exquisite chemical machines. However, we no more understand what mind and free will *are* today than did the ancient Greeks. This puzzle, the mind-body problem, has been the source of historic debate in the writings of many philosophers.

"It is not because they are composed of cells that we ascribe human minds to human beings. It is because of their behavior, which convinces each of us continually that they are like us in their ability to experience things, and in their self-awareness. And insofar as behavioral criteria are ultimately the practical basis for the recognition of mind, it must be admitted that androids *in no way* differ from biological humans.

"Your honor, the law must be based on objective criteria, open for all to inspect, and not on metaphysical doctrines. And the courts must so interpret the law. It is true that there are hard issues on which men of experience and wisdom may continue to differ, but these the law must not presume to decide. Any law that attempts to enshrine metaphysical doctrines must be declared void, for if we are not to base law on objective common experience, then we have abandoned our best means to settle disputes among men and nations.

"It must be recognized that the Princeton definition,

which has been cited in innumerable decisions, has held
that it is mind that defines a person. To injure the body is
battery, but to destroy the mind is murder. The words
contained in the Princeton document are 'cognitive function.' We believe we have shown that these words apply
equally to androids and humans, and that therefore by in-
ference, androids are persons under the Princeton definition.

"The defense has tried to show that androids are less
than human because they lack the abilities of extrasensory
perception. We believe we have refuted their contention.
Moreover, in the case of the brain of *Ozma II,* since it is
impossible to differentiate between the cognitive function
of the cellular part and that of the synthetic part, we
believe that the attempt to draw a distinction between
human and android cognition is entirely specious.

"In conclusion, we believe we have given every reason
to show why the writ of *mandamus* must be issued."

Carolyn sat down.

Litchfield stood and addressed the bench. He was
young, only about thirty, but had the facile glibness of a
politician, the ability to make a trivial statement sound
like a profound observation, to make nonsense seem plau-
sible.

"Your honor, the ramifications of this case go far
beyond the mere marriage of a man and a machine. A
decision in favor of the plaintiffs would threaten our entire way of life. By holding that androids are persons
under the law, you would be setting a precedent whose
consequences we can barely foresee. Androids would sue

to enter the sciences and professions, to own and transmit real property, to vote, and yes, even to run for office.

"As for love, there are many kinds of love as we all know, and the object of love is not always a person. A man may love his automobile, but the fact that a man loves a machine does not mean that the machine loves the man. In the present instance, the robot is merely doing what humans around it wish it to do. That is what these robots were designed for.

"A decision for the plaintiffs would raise essentially unsolvable questions. If androids are persons, why not invoice and billing computers, the telephone exchange, even sewing machines and typewriters? These examples may seem extreme, but if we do not draw the line between humans and machines, where *do* we draw it?

"At the other extreme, you and I know that technology knows no limits. If it were not for the deliberate mimicry of human faculties, why could there not be a race of super-androids, machines so extraordinary in their abilities as to make us despair of ever accomplishing anything of comparable significance? What is to keep machines from enslaving us, from becoming tyrants that can use us to their own ends and at their own whim?"

As we have used them, thought Paul.

Litchfield was perspiring as he paced in front of the bench. He began to lose hold of a disciplined line of reasoning. "What can we say to the poor father of a young woman who decides she wants to marry a robot? What about the enormous financial investment that society has in its robots? Who, indeed, will we get to perform the many jobs now held exclusively by androids when they are free to aspire to be artists, surgeons, yes, even lawyers and judges." He was squinting at Chloe Jackson. He began to pace again.

"Besides, androids look different in subtle ways. You can sometimes detect the odor of machine oil when they don't bathe."

Bullshit, thought Paul. Their plastic joints are self-lubricating, and their muscles are liquid crystal mechano-chemical transducers.

Litchfield was now standing directly in front of Judge Jackson, a handkerchief in one hand, his fingertips on the front of the bench. He went on.

"Your honor, androids never die unless they are destroyed. How can our brief tenure of six score years in this world compare with that? How can we be content to pass on, knowing that they and they alone may enjoy the gift of immortality?"

Paul felt a twinge at the reminder. But that is already the case, no matter what their legal status.

Litchfield was driving for a climax. "Besides, your honor, the issue at hand is not whether androids have *minds*, it is whether they have *souls*. If God had wanted man to be immortal, he would have made him so. No, He decreed that man must die to set his soul free. Come resurrection day, your honor, not one machine will rise from the grave to enter the Kingdom of Heaven!"

Litchfield sat down. Judge Jackson was impassive. She announced that she would take the case under advisement.

Three days later, on Monday, she read her decision in open court.

"First, as to matters of fact. I find the argument of the plaintiffs to be convincing. I find that androids are indeed persons. The argument raised by the defendant concerning the status of other devices of man's creation is not to be settled here, as this finding pertains only to the class of individuals directly concerned in this action. The demonstrations of telepathy, through dramatic, are not solely, nor even principally, the basis for this finding.

"Second, as to matters of law. Since androids are persons, they are entitled to the equal protection guaranteed by the Fourteenth Amendment to the Constitution. Therefore I grant plaintiffs' petition for a writ of *mandamus* requiring the clerk of this county immediately to issue a marriage license."

Judge Jackson rapped her gavel once, rose, and left the courtroom. On his way out, Litchfield stopped in front of Carolyn and said, "We're appealing."

"Not very," she replied.

·15·

FORWARD

"I HAVE NO CHILDREN *because I've been too busy,"* thought Paul.

"You have no children because you are afraid of death," thought Ben. "I'll show you." Through Ben's mind, Paul saw deeper into his own. "Many people have children as a hedge against mortality, but you've never believed it. To you, it is as though you would be admitting your own mortality by reproducing. You have reversed the usual line of reasoning."

"You have a child," thought Paul. "Your attitude must be different."

"Why should we be more alike than we are? Having children neither helps me nor hurts me in my struggle for survival, so why shouldn't I have a child? I just don't happen to subscribe to your fantasies."

This touching of the minds was fascinating to Paul, not only as an experience in itself, but because he was see-

ing in Ben what he might also have been, but wasn't.

"Why is it that you don't share the Clone Two fear and hatred of androids?" thought Paul.

"My father manufactured androids. I was raised by androids and have been around them ever since I can remember. A child accepts those things that make up its early experience as being utterly natural. Androids always seemed like people to me, long before I knew much else about the world, and this feeling must have dominated any latent hostilities I would otherwise have felt. Now that you have come to know androids as persons, your fear of them has also lessened. Perhaps you won't run away the next time you find yourself in bed with one."

Paul was shocked that Ben could dig out a memory that he himself was not conscious of at the moment. Ben laughed out loud.

Their minds merged more closely, more nearly becoming one. At will they could draw apart as distinct entities, or approach and lose themselves in a common union. They looked deeper into the unconscious, each helping the other. But as they approached total union, they became frightened and backed off, rising to the nominal level of linguistic, though unspoken, communication.

"What would happen if we went all the way?" thought Paul.

"What indeed? I'm afraid."

"Would we lock together permanently the way Fahy and the rest of Ozma have?"

Each looked and saw that he was a colony of personalities, or one, the perspective being a matter of choice. The partial integration of two originally separate minds had made clear the conventional nature of a person's assumption of his oneness.

"Our lives are paradoxes," thought Paul. "We both know that for us the world will end with our deaths. If there is no real future without immortality, why do we behave as though there were? How can I maintain my motivation to work? How can I do anything but indulge my animal appetites?"

"Perhaps we are merely sophisticated hedonists," replied Ben, "gratifying ourselves intellectually as well as sensually. I will probably live to satisfy my curiosity about the voyage to Tau Ceti. But you have altruistic motives as well as curiosity. Besides, for the first time there is immortality. There is a third mind among us. Marco is dead, but he lives on in you. At the moment of his death, you absorbed him. If memory means anything, if it means continuity and survival of self, then Marco lives on because you have his memories."

"Too bad we can't build android brains as much alike as the brains of the members of a human clone."

"It's never been tried. How much alike do they have to be before telepathic communication is possible? Ozma shows us that a commonality of past experience will suffice."

"It will be easier to develop more powerful android brains than human brains. Litchfield was right. They will be a step beyond us. Will they completely replace us? Should we build them?"

"Perhaps one day we will all be able to establish men-

tal contact, humans and androids. Ozma indicates that it's possible."

"But what if it isn't?"

"What have we ever transmitted to our children? What has any species passed on to its progeny? Information. It doesn't matter whether that information is genetic or cultural, does it?"

Paul found it hard to free himself from his biological prejudices, although he felt the force of the argument.

Ben went on. "Just as with the individual, it's the continuity of information, of states of knowledge and understanding, that defines the survival of a species or a culture. Its character may change drastically over the course of time, one species may evolve into another, but the lifeline is the continuity. So long as androids are conscious, they are a party to that continuity of culture and experience. No matter what one feels about personal immortality, they are our true children as surely as are the products of our eggs and sperms."

On December 3, the week after his letter appeared in *Nature*, Paul got a call from Amsterdam.

"Dr. Kyteler, this is Jan Hartsoeker, chairman of the Clonal Selection Commission. We are an affiliate of the World Health Organization, and we have the responsibility for the selection of clone recipients."

"I see."

"In fact, Dr. Kyteler, you are one of our most successful placements. I'm sorry if the secrecy surrounding your genetic antecedent has been a source of trouble to you. It was the wish of your parents."

"I think my personal problems are not the matter of primary concern."

"I'm pleased you feel that way. We are convening a special advisory panel on clones and extrasensory perception here in Amsterdam on December 20. We would like you to attend. We can cover your travel expenses and provide a small *per diem.*"

"Who else is attending?"

"All of our senior staff, and a representative of each of the twenty-eight clones."

"Of course I will attend. When should I arrive?"

"Any time on the nineteenth. Let us know your flight number, and we will meet you. Oh, I should add, in all candor, that our office has been contacted by both the Milan police and Interpol. They suspect that there is a connection between the clones and the civil disturbances of late."

When Paul stepped off the plane at Amsterdam, it was cold and raining. A limousine and chauffeur were waiting to take him to the concrete and glass building that housed the central body bank and the offices and laboratories of the Commission. It was very formal and polite, with a cocktail mixer for all of the guests who had arrived. They had accommodations on the top floor of the building itself.

At nine the next morning they convened in a lecture hall on the second floor. There was a series of brief papers by staff members on the history and current status of the clones. The technical aspects of cloning were reviewed in some detail for the nonbiologists. Apparently Paul was the only member of the group of visitors who had not known the nature of his origin since childhood. It was pointed out the Commission shunned publicity because the number of applicants for cloned children far exceeded the number of clone births the Commission wished to authorize. Clone recipients were screened largely on the basis of their emotional stability and on the likelihood that they would provide a stimulating home environment for the children. As evidence of a generally conservative philosophy, very few of the clone recipients were unmarried women. Although other groups had successfully experimented with *in vitro* embryogenesis in humans using artificial placentas, the cloning program had never authorized any but normal intra-uterine development.

Several studies were reported concerning the medical problems of the clones. It turned out that four clones had a predisposition to cancer. One in particular, in which forty percent of the members developed melanomas, had been studied in great detail. Another study indicated that two clones were prone to schizophrenia, only one being of the chemically manageable type. The problems had not, of course, developed in the progenitors at the times their respective clones were founded. These investigations greatly extended the earlier identical twin studies on the relative roles of heredity and environment in the development of disease. The one clone that gave rise to untreatable psychosis had been terminated insofar as new births were concerned.

There was only one recorded case of an organ transplant rejection between two members of the same clone. It was determined that a bacterial infection the donor had contracted before his accidental death had introduced new antigens into his cell surfaces which were the source of the graft rejection.

One of the staff psychologists presented the results of a study on the scholastic achievement, I.Q., personality development, career choices, and life styles of members of several clones. The result was that there was a high correlation within each clone, in all but the last two categories. Although most of the individuals were highly productive and creative, the methods and fields they chose to express this creativity depended more on their environmental experiences than on their genetic makeup.

The high point of the morning was a presentation by the senior staff statistician. He had extracted data from the literature on learning behavior in rats. It showed that the number of trials necessary for an animal to learn a task dropped by about two-thirds during the time cloned rats were replacing inbred strain rats in research laboratories. A detailed examination of the results of several experiments showed that, within given experimental groups, later rats tended to do significantly better than earlier rats with regard to first trials. The most likely explanation seemed to be the transmission of learned information through telepathic communication among rats.

The last event of the morning was a short address by Hartsoeker. He noted that ESP had been considered a possibility from the outset, as a result of the views expressed by Enzo Cigala.

They recessed for lunch and reconvened in a large paneled seminar room at two-thirty. After making it clear how serious a problem they faced, Hartsoeker introduced the representative from Interpol. The threat implied by his presence was felt by everyone. Hartsoeker asked for discussion. Paul spoke first.

"One thing that you should realize, and I can speak only for the Clone Twos, is that we did not know we were telepathic. Not a single Clone Two, other than myself, retained any conscious recollection of engaging in sociopathic activity. And there were apparently no other times at which mental contact was established."

The Clone Nine from Tokyo responded. "Yes, I think that is so. I myself never knew the significance of what happened in Kyoto, and I have never experienced ESP, to my knowledge."

Hartsoeker cleared his throat. He was sitting at the head of the long table with a large abstract bronze sculpture suspended from the ceiling behind him. They all turned to face him. He coughed into his handkerchief and put it in his pocket. "But Dr. Kyteler, the memorandum you distributed this morning indicates that you saw these events in your sleep, and moreover, you obviously displayed voluntary telepathic union with Dr. Rose."

"All of the Clone Twos except Dr. Rose and me live in Western Europe. At the time of the July riot, we were both asleep. Dr. Rose has no recollection of that event, but he and other Clone Twos also report strange dreams during the past several years. Apparently one is much more susceptible to receiving ESP during sleep."

The Clone Twenty-one representative spoke up in a heavy Russian accent. "I am still not satisfied, Dr. Kyteler, that you have fully explained why you, and not others, have telepathy while in a normal waking state."

"The Clone Twos are now all able to initiate and terminate telepathic contact at will. This seems to be a second stage in the development of the ability."

Hartsoeker looked worried. "Gentlemen and ladies, I am not sure this helps us toward a solution of the problem we face. Are there any suggestions?"

Several people started to speak simultaneously, but Paul stood and drew their attention. "After a meeting of the minds, so to speak," he had to wait for the laughter to subside, "the Clone Twos became convinced that we could develop a strong enough awareness, or superego, to control our actions. It is rather like the socialization of a child. The corporate mind has to learn to establish direction over the emotional outbursts that are its first form of expression. We can assure you that there will never be a repetition of a Clone Two riot."

The representative from Interpol spoke. "I believe you mean that, but what if this 'corporate control' fails, Dr. Kyteler?"

A staff neurochemist answered: "In the last two weeks, we have been running preliminary tests here in my laboratory on Clone Twos. It appears that there are several psychotropic drugs in common use, such as the THC series, that can completely inhibit telepathic interaction."

The Clone Four representative, a member of the group that had rioted in Geneva, broke in sarcastically. She addressed the man from Interpol. "What do you plan to do? Round us up and put us in detention camps? There would be a hell of a stink if you did that, you know. Many of the clone members are very important and respected people in their own countries."

"Interpol will not take any action ourselves, of course, but we have discussed various contingency plans with the representatives of several countries. In some cases, legislative authorization would be necessary before such detentions could take place. There has been a great deal of concern. The fact that it has not been reported in the press should not be misinterpreted by any of you."

Hartsoeker took over from him. "Several governments have already asked us to refrain from any further cloning procedures until the situation is clarified. We have tentatively agreed to a two-year moratorium, and in turn have gained the concession that no action will be taken against clone members, even those who have committed criminal acts. It comes to this: we have two years to prove that we can effectively police ourselves. Otherwise, outside intervention is inevitable. This means, among other things, that any clone unable to establish complete control over itself will be terminated, and the present members will be dispersed around the world to take advantage of the distance effect. If this fails, whatever stronger measures are needed will be taken. I have already given my word on this. The situation is more critical than you might imagine, since most clones have yet to experience ESP. Perhaps they will not, but I think they will. Without sufficient advance preparation and surveillance, the initial acts following first telepathic contact could be disastrous. Therefore we are going to attempt to initiate telepathy within each clone, under controlled conditions, here in the laboratories in this building."

The man from Interpol spoke again. "An international conference on the status of androids is being called in a few months. It looks as though other countries will follow the lead of the United States and recognize the rights of androids. You all realize that this will make the killing of an android an act of murder."

The Russian Clone Twenty-one returned to the point he had raised earlier. "Dr. Kyteler, do you insist that your unique role in these events in no way indicates that you are different from other Clone Twos?"

Paul paused before answering. "I suspect that I *am* different from the other Clone Twos. We all know that viral infections can permanently alter the genetic composition of a host organism. I have synthesized hundreds of human transduction genes in my work, and I wouldn't be surprised if most of them were floating around in my own cells right now."

There was polite laughter around the table.

"Nevertheless," continued Paul, "I think my role was largely a matter of chance."

The consensus was that the problems could be controlled and that the cloning program should be pressed forward after the two-year pause. There was, however, more conviction in some faces than others.

When the meeting broke and it was time to leave, Paul recalled that he had bought only a one-way ticket when he left Cleveland. The closer his limousine got to Amsterdam airport, the more clearly he understood what he was going to do. He purchased a ticket to Milan. Today Marco was going home to Alexa and Tullio.

The flight was quiet and uneventful, and he took a taxi from the airport to Alexa's apartment. It was dark and no one was home. He carried his bags to a nearby café where he ordered a drink. After a while he walked back to Alexa's place. The lights were on, and he thought he heard voices inside. He knocked at the door. The voices stopped, but no one came to answer. He knocked several times again. Still no one came. He backed up and tried to look into the window, but the curtains were drawn across it. So he sat down on his suitcase and waited. It was dark and the wind was making him feel very cold. His stomach began to hurt, and he had a terrible feeling of anxiety. He was giving up his laboratory in the States to live with Alexa, and she wouldn't even let him in.

He crossed his arms in front of him to keep warm, and then he thought, perhaps she's moved and this is no longer her apartment. Perhaps it's someone else who won't answer the door. He got up, took his bags, and began to walk. He reached his old apartment, tried the key he had kept, and the door opened. The rooms smelled musty, but it was warm. He touched the light switch and found that the electricity was still on. He realized that Tullio must have been keeping his place up for him in the hope that he would return. He dialed Alexa's number. The phone rang for a long time before there was an answer. Marco could hear the sound of music playing at the other end.

"Hello?"

"Alexa, it's Marco." For a moment there was silence.

"Marco?" Her voice was strained. He could hear a man's voice, and Alexa covered the phone so he could not hear what was being said. "Marco, where are you?"

"I'm here, in Milan, in my apartment." His heart was racing. "Alexa, let me come over. I want to talk to you."

"You can't, Marco. Not now." There was a long silence.

"Why?"

"Don't ask. We can talk later."

Marco knew she had been making love to the man in her apartment. He felt a terrible frustration. "Alexa, come out and meet me. I love you so much. Won't you come and meet me?"

She began to cry and put her hand over the phone. Then she said, "Marco, I can't talk to you now. I can't talk at all."

"All right, if that's what you want."

"Yes."

"Goodbye."

"Goodbye."

He hung up and sat down in a chair. Then he got up and went out into the street, and walked until he was standing across from Alexa's apartment. A few minutes later the door opened, and he saw two figures in the lighted doorway. Alexa shook her head no. The man said something, and she shook her head no again. The man took a step backward, facing her, and Alexa closed the door. The man stood there for a while, then he turned and came down the street in Marco's direction. Marco looked at him as he went by. He was thin, with sharp features and intense eyes. He walked quickly down the street.

Marco went back to his apartment, took out a bottle of red wine, opened it, and drank it all without sitting down. After a few minutes everything looked softer, his stomach felt better, and the anguish began to subside. He turned on the radio to some music, went into the bathroom, and looked in the mirror. His face looked like a stranger's. The features seemed to shift and move as he stared. His eyes frightened him, and he turned away. He opened another bottle of wine and began to drink. Halfway through he started gagging but he forced himself to finish it, then turned off the lights, and looked out the window. He felt very sorry for himself, so he locked the door and staggered around, banging into things, until he fell on the bed. When he closed his eyes the room spun, but he felt warm and comfortable.

In the morning he had, of course, a terrible hangover. He got up, opened his suitcase and changed clothes. Now that he realized he was actually Paul, and not Marco, he felt foolish about the lapse of the previous evening. He was sad about Alexa, but knew that she had to be free to follow her own life. He started planning what he would do when he got back to Cleveland. Even though he had been gone only a few days, he was already wondering about what had been happening in his lab. He would go out and try to eat something, and then phone for a flight back to the U.S.

When he opened the door to go out, he saw a note taped to it: "Marco, I suppose it's better if we don't see each other anymore. Alexa."

Immediately his heart began to pound, and his face became flushed. He ran all the way to Alexa's apartment and knocked on the door as hard as he could. A voice asked, "Who is it?"

"It's Marco."

"Marco, what do you want?"

"Alexa, open the door. I have to talk to you for a minute."

She unlocked the door, opened it a little, and peeked out. Her eyes were red, and she looked as though she hadn't slept. He pushed the door open and stepped in. She was wearing a white shift.

"Alexa, I love you."

"How can you? You're not even Marco."

"Yes, I am. I really am. How can you doubt it?"

"You didn't even say goodbye when you left. That's twice you've done that. It's just too cruel."

"You're not being fair." Marco knew that she was on the defensive about last night. He was going to remind her that the reason he didn't say goodbye the first time was that he had died. But he didn't say anything.

She looked away from him and her voice was very shaky. "I phoned you back last night, I don't know how many times. I called and called, but you wouldn't answer. Then I went down and pounded on your door, and on your window, and called to you, but you wouldn't let me in. I know you were there. I was crying and making so much noise, I can't imagine what your neighbors must think."

"Alessandra, I couldn't hear you."

"Of course you could. Everyone in the neighborhood could. You just wouldn't answer your phone or let me in."

"After I talked to you last night I drank two bottles of wine and passed out. Nothing could have got me up."

They looked at each other, and they both had tears in their eyes. Alexa reached out to him. He took her in his arms, and they held on to each other as hard as they could.